# THE NEUSTRIAN PRINCESS

by
Donald Brown

**Special Thanks**

I would like to thank Lauren Etchells, another Jersey writer, for her editorial assistance and cover illustrations.

## PROLOGUE

In the banqueting hall of the Neustrian imperial palace, the conference lasted all morning. After a heavy lunch, punctuated by toasts and tedious speeches, the young Empress Prunella, known to her only friend as 'Prue', followed the guests and notables through an arched doorway in the glass frontage and down the steps onto the veranda. Her stepmother wasn't watching. Good! She and her sister were still chatting to their strange guests from the isles beyond the sea.

She slipped away from the throng and rested her arms on the marble balustrade, staring beyond the lawn and the beach, towards those far-off islands tossed like stones in the northern ocean. If you put them all together, she knew that those islands wouldn't cover half the space of what should have been her Neustrian Empire.

She felt the vast might of that empire stretching behind her; the wheat fields and rivers and forests, sprinkled with towns and villages that she had visited on horseback with her father in the year before he died. All this was hers, she thought. Except that it wasn't. She was just a prisoner in her own palace, 'protected'- 'for her own good, of course!' - by her scheming stepmother and her odious younger sister. She missed her father terribly. She had only a fleeting memory of her mother, who'd died when she was only three, but her father had always been there for her and taught her all the important things she knew. It seemed so tragic and unfair that a man so strong and healthy could die, just like that, from the sting of a bee.

She looked longingly out to sea. Could the stranger's arrival offer a means of escape? He hadn't explained what he had come for. Her stepmother had planned it that way. The whole point of those boring, ceremonial speeches was to keep her counsellors in the dark. She'd shoo them away soon and invite the young man to a meeting in her private council chamber. That's when the real talks would begin. Prunella kicked the balustrade in anger and winced when she remembered she was only wearing sandals. She had to attend that meeting! After all, the young man had a ship. If she played her cards skilfully, he might offer to take her with him.

She had read a lot about those western isles. That was all part of her training to become an Empress, which had stopped suddenly on her fourteenth birthday when her father died and her stepmother took over. She knew some of her own ancestors had once settled in those isles. Nowadays they were called 'colonists' and the natives, because they had brown skin and attacked the invaders on ships, were called 'pirates.'

She thought she would like the pirates better. She knew they had a 'Guardian' about the same age as herself, called 'Josh.' He was an epileptic who was incredibly brave and had visionary powers, which enabled him to defeat the colonists and put an end to the recent war. But then he'd confirmed the peace by surrendering the three stones which harnessed his visionary powers to the Temple of Harmony. That was a big mistake!

The visitor was a pirate too. He was tall and handsome, with a soft, thoughtful voice, and sad, dark eyes. He wore a long, white tunic edged with purple, like a priest, but he claimed to be descended from a Prince, so he was probably a warrior too. He'd only brought two companions with him, who wore strange iron helmets that reached right down to their necks. They never said a word unless spoken to, and then looked at him, as if they needed his approval before they replied. She thought he must be more important than he seemed.

She looked round and gasped when she saw that the crowd on the veranda had dispersed. She spotted her stepmother and her younger sister scurrying towards their private council chamber next to the assembly room. The Prince with his companions was not far behind, but he stopped when he saw her striding towards him and waited for her to catch up. She increased her stride, doing up the top button of her pink blouse and smoothing down her fair wind-blown hair as she approached him. "I would love to know about your plans," she explained with a smile.

"You are the Empress," he said, regarding her with interest. "You have a right to know."

Her stepmother pursed her lips with fury when she saw her. She stood at the door of the chamber like a porcelain doll, a small woman – smaller than Prunella - with short black hair and bright beady eyes, and a quick, precise way of talking. She greeted the Prince and his companions with a flurry of compliments, asking them to call her Lucinda, and remarking on the trouble the Prince had taken to cross the seas to greet them. Her younger sister, Laetitia, who was almost a head taller and had long bleach-blond hair, breathed similar compliments in her soft lisping voice. She held onto the Prince's hand and assured him, as she gazed into his eyes, that they were both 'absolutely longing to hear his proposals.'

At this point, Lucinda turned to Prunella and said in a polite voice edged with steel, "Prunella dear, I have good news for you. You've had a long morning and now you need a rest. Your presence won't be needed at this meeting. Besides, you aren't really dressed for this sort of thing, are you?"

Prunella looked down at her sandals and jeans, which she'd worn as a gesture of rebellion, and pretended not to understand. "The Prince has asked me to come," she said.

Before her stepmother could respond, the Prince announced in his soft, clear voice. "I am afraid I must insist on her presence. You see, the future is an open book, and we never know with whom I may have to deal in the future."

Prunella suppressed a smile. That Prince had a nerve! She was beginning to like him! She cast a sideways glance at her stepmother, whose look suggested she was ready to cancel the meeting. In the end, curiosity forced her to swallow her pride. "Well, of course, if you insist," she sighed, darting a look at Prunella which suggested she'd pay for this insistence. They were soon comfortably seated in armchairs round an oval table; the Prince and his companions on one side, close to the door, Lucinda and Laetitia on the other side, and Prunella at the far end between Laetitia and the Prince.

"My proposal is very simple," the Prince began, smiling at her stepmother. "I know your lands are extensive – the lands that your Empress will no doubt inherit when she comes of age."

Did he realise the effect those words would have on her stepmother? Something about his calm demeanour suggested that he did realise! Did that mean he would rather deal with her? She imagined the expression on her stepmother's face but kept her head down, afraid to look.

"I suppose your expenses must be considerable," the Prince continued, "employing men to plough your fields and soldiers to keep your realm in order."

Prunella could see that her stepmother had started to soften towards him. Money – and the lack of it – was her favourite topic of conversation. She fastened her bright eyes on the Prince and said with a sigh, "Everything's so expensive nowadays."

The Prince returned her smile. "I have come here to make you an offer," he said, "one that will provide you with manpower at minimal expense – men whose loyalty you can command at the click of a switch." He pointed to the two members of his crew humbly seated by his side. "You will notice that the skin colour of my friends is not brown like mine, but pink like your own."

Lucinda gave a little laugh, growing a little pinker as she corrected him. "White!" she said. "We call it white!"

"Let's call it white then," said the Prince. "The point I would like to make is that my friends here are colonists like yourselves. As I'm sure you are aware, a very long time ago – nearly four hundred years, I believe – a group of colonists left your lands and came and settled in the Western Isles."

"Trouble- makers!" snorted Lucinda.

The Prince nodded. He turned to the giant on his left, a head taller than his colleague.

"Would you say you were a trouble-maker, Osborne?" he asked.

"I done trouble," said Osborne. "But I won't do trouble no more. I been re-educated."

"Let's put it to the test," said the Prince. He placed a small black disc on the table and said, "If I ask you to make trouble now, what will you say?"

Osborne hesitated and then replied, "I'd say 'no.'"

"Wrong answer, I'm afraid," said the Prince. "If I ask you to make trouble, you do as I command you."

Osborne's eyes widened in horror, and he began to tremble with fear.

The Prince leaned over the table and pressed one of the three small buttons on the disc. Osborne gave an almighty groan and his massive frame began to shake.

"Switch that thing off!" he sobbed as he fell forward, elbows resting on the table.

After a few seconds, the Prince pressed another button and Osborne heaved a great sigh and sat back in the chair, breathing heavily.

Laetitia gave a little squeal of excitement. "Can I have a go with that thing?" she asked.

"Laetitia, please!" her sister cried in a cross voice. "This thing is not a toy!"

The Prince's eyes gleamed with delight. "I see you and I are of one mind," he said. "To tell you the truth," he went on, gazing at Lucinda as if truth were embedded in his nature, "I very rarely use this device."

"I suppose it saves electricity; not to use it all the time, I mean," said Laetitia, staring at the Prince with her wide blue eyes, like a love-struck fan.

"The fact that I can use it is enough," said the Prince. "Isn't that right, Osborne?"

"Whatever you say, boss," said Osborne, struggling for an answer that would save him from another bout of agony.

The Prince smiled.

Prunella did what she'd learned to do for over a year; hide her feelings behind a mask of innocence. Her sudden liking for the Prince had crashed to the floor. He was rotten to the core – worse even than her stepmother! She guessed why he might want her on that ship. He would want her as a tool – no more – someone dumb enough to follow his orders; not hold out for a higher price, as would certainly be the case with her stepmother. Well, she'd join him if he asked, but she'd find a way of losing him at the first port of call.

"Tell me more about your proposal," said Lucinda, placing a notepad on her lap.

"In a little while," said the Prince. "I am proposing to send you my first batch of colonists; two hundred men and women to work as slaves on your estates, and all I ask in return is a similar number of drones. Those artificial bees that pollinate your crops."

Prunella shot a dark glance at her stepmother.

"Will the slaves be wearing helmets?" asked Lucinda.

"I always feel that obedience is a virtue," said the Prince. "Don't you feel the same, Osborne?"

Prunella had heard enough. She couldn't stay one minute longer in that room without betraying her unease. She forced a smile and stood up. "I wish you well with your venture," she said to the Prince, "and I hope we will meet again soon. I don't think you need me for the next bit as it sounds too technical for my poor brain, so I hope you won't mind if I take my leave."

Once out of the door, she made a dash for her bedroom, packed her bags, and headed through the woods where nobody could see her, to the harbour where the ship was moored. With any luck, the Prince would welcome her on board. And, with a bit more luck, she could slip off the boat at the first port of call and meet up with the Pirate Guardian.

# CHAPTER ONE

Cycling home from another great party in the centre of town, Josh kept his head down and pedalled hard along the wide, lighted avenue lined with orange trees and bougainvillea, his brain spinning with the sights and smells of this small, southern island. A warm, tropical breeze ruffled his hair as he headed out of town.

He rose in his seat to gain speed. Feathers would feel bound to wait up for him. That's what would annoy the old man most. Megs too. He pictured her black eyes smouldering with reproach. He should have 'left earlier' when some of his friends left. Megs had suddenly become the responsible one, though she was a good year younger than himself.

His legs ached as he pedalled up the steep gradient towards the dimly lit outskirts of town. He knew the old man worried about his safety - but he didn't feel afraid in Amaryllis. Being the Pirate Guardian made him a bit of a celebrity. He liked the way people recognised him on the streets and called out to him. Still, he felt bad about Feathers. He looked down at the road sliding back beneath his pedalling feet. Not much further to go. He had reached the top of the hill by the lighted monument and was freewheeling now along the dark stretch of road that curved downwards past the docks and up again towards the pink and white holiday bungalows that lined the coast.

He didn't have any lights on his bicycle. Nobody seemed to mind in Amaryllis, but he could barely see what lay in front of him. He put his head down and pedalled hard through this murky area of wasteland and dimly lit estates. He'd been stopped more than once by strangers stepping out in front of him, begging or threatening. He usually swerved past them, ignoring their jeers as he sped on out of sight. Tonight, he heard nothing – only the sound of raucous celebrations from the lighted centre of town behind him.

He heard the roar of a motorbike from the top of the hill by the monument. He'd noticed those motor bikes, revving their engines up and down outside the house where the party was being held. Another roar followed. Then they all started, like cocks competing for their kingdom.

He fixed his eyes on the kerb and the shadows of the docks beyond. The next street on his left was Mile End Road, the last and oldest street in town, a narrow, cobbled lane of small, terraced houses leading down to the docks. He always passed it in a hurry. It looked like the kind of street to avoid after dark.

The roar of the motorbikes had grown louder. They had almost caught up with him. He welcomed their company and slowed up a little, hugging the kerb to leave room for them to overtake. To his surprise, they slowed down too. They'd cut their engines and opted to fall in line behind him.

That didn't feel right. Bikers liked to laugh and josh one another. These guys just hung on his tail; a whole gang of them. He pedalled on, expecting them at any moment to roar past him. Instead, they slowed up. Their silence began to unnerve him. What were they waiting for? His eyes scanned the road for a possible escape route. The semi-darkness stretched ahead for about a mile. He pressed hard on the pedals.

Then a rough voice from the back of the group shouted, "Josh? That your name? Josh?" The unfriendly tone shot a wave of tension down his neck and shoulders. He tightened his grip on the handlebars. Another, younger, voice right behind him said, "Yea, that's him." He pedalled hard, eyes scanning the side of the road for a bolthole.

Suddenly, two bikes roared past, nearly knocking him off his bike as they brushed past him, pushing him into the kerb and swerving round to block him off. Others pressed him from behind, one of them bumping his back wheel. His heart beat furiously as he gripped his handlebars, hunting for a plan of escape.

A huge guy in a black leather jacket dismounted and loomed over him, blocking his escape. In a dreamlike trance of fear, Josh stared at the letters 'RR', picked out in white on the man's chest.

The man raised one hand to his mates, who laughed and went silent. He looked down at Josh. "Phone!" he said, holding out a hand to receive it.

Josh was in a place where he didn't want to be, late at night, in a deserted part of town. With sweaty hands, he fumbled for his phone. If this was a mugging, maybe they'd let him go. The man gave him a hard stare, took the phone and smashed it against the handlebars, tossing the pieces behind him. Josh gulped. He felt himself drowning in a sea of hostile faces.

The guy let go of his handlebars. "We're taking you down to the docks," he said, "for a little talk." The others laughed.

That did it. Josh slipped off his bike and ran.

Amid shouts and muffled curses, he stumbled over the grass verge and raced down the nearest side street. Behind him he heard sounds of a hasty conference; the big guy giving orders and the rest, who seemed to be younger, falling into line. His dash for freedom must have taken them by surprise, because he heard no immediate attempt to follow him. Then, as he raced down the dark, narrow street, he saw why they took their time. They'd forced him left off the avenue, down Mile End Road. Some of them were revving up their bikes and heading off – they'd sweep round to meet him at the docks!

He glanced round to see two shadows, including the heavy shape of the man he feared most, making their slow, purposeful descent. Sweating now, he raced down the dark, narrow street, desperate to put more space between himself and his pursuers.

He heard their heavy boots clattering on the cobbles behind him. They didn't sound in a hurry. They knew he had nowhere to go. As he ran, his eyes darted from side to side, searching for an alleyway that offered a means of escape. On either side, an unbroken line of dark, terraced houses stretched down towards that murky space where the street ended, and the rest of their gang would lie in wait. His two pursuers followed at a distance, like beaters driving him into a trap.

Panting, he saw a single lighted window halfway down the street; then another light on the other side; and another. He raced towards the lights. There must be hundreds of people crammed into those tiny houses, all asleep. An army of people! If only they could help him! Maybe, if he started ringing doorbells, somebody would let him in. He'd reached the lights by now and tried one door, then another. He looked round. His pursuers had made no effort to catch up. He listened for their footfalls and saw their dark shapes in the distance; just two of them, but bigger than him and probably armed with knives. Still, he stood a better chance against those two than facing the whole gang at the end of the street. Except one of them was that big guy with 'RR' on his chest! 'RR' – Rupert the Rebel. This was no ordinary biker.

He felt in his pockets for a weapon, but he didn't even have a penknife. Then he saw a few loose cobbles at the side of the street. Not much use against that guy, but it made him feel better holding one in each hand. He picked them up.

Then he had a better idea. He stopped and tossed one of the cobbles at a lighted window. He heard a tinkle of glass and saw a few scattered shards fall at his feet. They might not answer doors, these people, but surely a broken window would get some reaction! He looked up. No sound. Nothing. His pursuers saw what he was up to and quickened their pace. He put the other cobble in his right hand and aimed at the next house, but fumbled and missed.

The two bikers had broken into a run. He fumbled around for more stones and tried again. Another tinkle of glass. And the next. What was it with these people? He expected lights to go on and angry faces to peer out of their windows. His pursuers were hurrying now, but he knew he could outrun them if he tried. He gathered all the stones he could hold and flung them up at the windows on his own side of the street.

A light went on in the window opposite. A wave of hope washed over him. He waited with clenched fists for the window to open. Another light shone in the window next door and a voice called "Hoy!"

He felt a huge release of tension, hearing that angry voice shouting at him from the window where he'd thrown the first stone. "Hoy!" Then another window opened. The bikers stood in the shadows, watching. From the first house, a large bald man in a brown dressing gown stuck his head out of the window. "You've broken my window!" he shouted.

"He's broken mine too!" cried a shrill voice from the house next door.

"You just wait, young man," bellowed another voice from the house behind him. "I'm coming after you!"

*Let him come soon!*

"You've broken my window!" repeated the bald man in the dressing gown.

Josh stepped into the middle of the street in full view of the lighted window. For a moment, those men looked poised to make a dash from the shadows and grab him, but they hung back. He looked up at the windows. "I can explain!" he shouted.

"Hang on a minute, Ed!" cried the shrill voice. "I know that young man. He's the Pirate Guardian."

"I don't care if he's the Pirate King, Nora!" cried the first voice. "He's broken my window."

"Pirates don't have kings," said the shrill voice. "They have princes, and they have Guardians. Besides, he says he can explain."

"Explain what? He's broken my window. Anyway, we don't have proper Guardians anymore; leastways not ones that go round breaking windows."

Josh gasped as a brawny arm tightened its hold round his windpipe. "The police will be here in a minute," said the man from the house behind him, giving his windpipe another squeeze. "You'll see."

"He's famous!" cried the shrill voice. "Lay off of him, Bill. You're choking him." More front doors opened, and their owners spilled out onto the street. Josh grinned as he saw his pursuers edging away from the scene. The grip on his throat relaxed, and he found himself surrounded. Some of the onlookers, mostly women, took the side of the shrill voice. "Let go of his neck," they cried. "He's only a lad! You're throttling him!" Others inclined to the male side of the argument; "He's broken my window!" roared the first voice, "and yours too," he added as an afterthought.

"He says he can explain," said the shrill voice.

"He can explain all he wants, and when he's finished, I'll hit him," said the man with the arm round Josh's neck.

"They tried to kill me," said Josh, seizing his chance to move the conversation along a bit.

"Who tried to kill you?"

"That's no excuse for breaking my window!"

"Hang on! I said who tried to kill him?"

"He could have knocked on my door."

"Pull the other one, Bill! When's the last time you ever opened the door to a stranger at night?"

"Well, I didn't see anyone trying to kill him."

"That's because you were asleep!"

Josh found himself surrounded by curious faces. "I wanted to wake you up so that you could save my life," he shouted. The crowd had stopped talking now, so he lowered his voice. "I'm sorry about the windows but I was being chased by a gang on motorbikes." Some of the onlookers cast doubtful stares up and down the street. "They chased me up the avenue," he said. "They had RR printed on their jackets – Rupert the Rebel. They left their motor bikes up there and followed me here on foot. The rest are waiting for me by the docks."

The crowd went silent. He felt the arm being released from his neck. "Bikers!" said the man, shaking the stiffness out of his arm. "You know what, lad? You've given me a cramp," he added, as if it was Josh's fault that he'd hurt his arm trying to strangle him. His neighbours waited. He was clearly a bit of a leader in that street. "Bikers!" he snorted. "We know that lot! Come on, young man. I think we'd better get you home."

"What about the police?" asked the shrill voice.

"I didn't call them, did I? What policeman would lose sleep over a broken window in Mile End Road?"

Josh heard murmurs of agreement. He found himself among friends. Bit by bit, as they accompanied him back to the avenue, they pieced together the story of the young Pirate Guardian being waylaid by a gang of bikers in the pay of the Rebel Prince. They found his bike where he'd left it, lying with its wheels up on the side of the avenue. They even insisted on walking him part of the way home until he reached the line of pink and white bungalows where he mounted his bicycle and pedalled off up the lighted avenue that led to his home. He laid his bike against the wall of the bungalow and shrugged off the events of the night. Next came the difficult bit. He tapped lightly on the front door.

Megs came to the door and held up a hand to caution him against going inside. "Sh! Feathers is asleep," she warned him.

"What time did he fall asleep?" whispered Josh.

"Ten o'clock."

She noticed his relief. Her face darkened. "Look, you're not getting away with this, Josh!"

"They tried to kill me."

"Seriously?"

"Yes, seriously! Bikers. One of them had 'RR' printed on his jacket. They probably all did, but I couldn't see in the dark."

Her eyes widened. She tugged his arm and said, "Come on. Let's go inside."

They sat opposite each other at the kitchen table.

"They smashed my phone and chased me down Mile End Road," Josh explained. He told her about the chase. She giggled when he got to the bit about the broken windows. But when he'd finished, she gave him a solemn look and shook her head. "What time did you leave the party?" She asked.

"I don't know. About twelve."

Megs gave a wry smile. "Come on, Josh," she said. "You know exactly. You're always looking at your watch. What time was it?"

He hesitated. "12h30," he admitted. "Why does it matter?"

"For goodness' sake, Josh! Your mum would go crazy if she knew. Why else did your parents send us to Amaryllis? It's meant to be safe for you here, but nowhere is completely safe at that time of night."

He shrugged. He didn't have an answer to that one.

She leaned back and smiled. "Tell me about the party," she said. "Were many people there?"

He knew where this question was leading. "Some of my year group," he said.

"Was Sharon there?" she asked

"Yea, some of the time."

"What's she like?"

"I don't know. All right."

"Did you kiss her?"

"Yea, sort of."

"Only sort of?" She gave a mischievous grin.

He remembered Sharon's kiss, her soft lips seeking his with sudden knowingness in the darkened room. He tried to shake the memory away.

"What are we going to do about those bikers?" Megs asked. "Tell your parents?"

"No way. They'd probably call us home or ask for a 24-hour guard on the house and Feathers would go mental. Can you imagine? We've got to work this one out by ourselves."

To his surprise, she nodded. "The Prince wants to kill you," she said finally. "We know that at least. He can't claim to rule the pirate world while people are still running around saying. Look, there's Josh! He's our Guardian!"

Josh felt as if he'd opened a door into a dark space. "What can I do? If the Prince is still out to get me, he has spies everywhere – even on Amaryllis. So I won't be safe until someone kills him, which doesn't look like happening."

Megs nodded and got up from the table. "Poor boy!" she said. "We'll think of something. Let's talk some more in the morning."

## CHAPTER TWO

J osh stumbled down to breakfast, grabbed a bowl and cereal from the sideboard and sat hunched at the table, spooning food in the general direction of his face. The sun blazed through the kitchen window. He checked his watch; nearly eleven o'clock.

Feathers stumped into the kitchen, with a rolled- up newspaper in one hand. "Good party, was it?" he asked.

Josh looked up. "Very good, thanks."

Feathers stood facing him across the table. "Just you be careful, my lad."

"Yes, of course."

"Because the Prince is back in action again." Feathers tossed his copy of 'The Daily Trumpeter' on the table. His blue eyes looked strained.

Josh sat up in shock. Had Feathers heard something about the previous night? "What's he done?" he asked, trying to sound casual.

Feathers scratched the grey curls at the top of his beard. "Never mind what he's done," he said. "It's what he's going to do that worries me. Believe me, there are a lot of pirates – even here in Amaryllis – that support his campaign. So you've got to be careful where you go – especially at night. I don't want you getting attacked!"

Josh hid his face in the newspaper. "I'll be careful!" he mumbled.

The old man slowly shook his head. "I don't know. Still, on a brighter note, take a look at the back page."

Josh turned over the paper. His eyes fell on the photo of a girl with silky, black hair and bright, mischievous eyes, sitting side-saddle on a wall, staring out to sea. She wore blue jeans, a white blouse and a red piratical scarf. "Why, that's Megs!" he exclaimed. "She never told me!"

"Yes, she's been selected by the tourist board to represent our island. Her picture will be in all the travel agencies."

"But that's brilliant!"

"Yes," mused Feathers. "It's a good choice when you come to think of it. Look at her! She's just the kind of daughter that every traditional pirate family would like to have; bright, attractive, feisty!" He looked round. "Better not sing her praises too highly," he whispered.

Megs stood in the doorway. An embarrassed smile crept over her face as she saw the back page in Josh's hands. "I only entered that competition for a joke," she said, "but it turned out great because I get to go on tours and stuff, and they pay for some of my clothes."

"I don't know how I'll cope," grumbled Feathers, "having two celebrities in the house. One's bad enough!"

Megs came and put an arm over the old man's shoulders. "Come on Feathers! At least we share the housework and help with the cooking." She mouthed a question at Josh behind Feathers' back. In answer, he stood up. "We're going into town," he explained to Feathers. "We'll do the food shopping and maybe call on some friends. We won't be long!"

They hurried out of the house before Feathers had time to protest, walking into the brilliant midday heat. Josh felt a lightness in his step as he followed Megs down the familiar pavement which curved downwards past the pink and white bungalows towards the tall-masted sailing ships with their crimson sails anchored in the bay.

"Lucy was round here this morning. You just missed her," said Megs. "I haven't seen her for ages; not since her mum started that farm shop. We went shopping together. We had loads to talk about."

"Yea."

He regretted not seeing more of Lucy since she'd come to Amaryllis. She was the girl who'd given him the central stone in the Guardian's necklace. Now she and her parents lived in a cottage in the woods, an hour's walk up the road from Feathers' bungalow. "What did you talk about?" he asked suspiciously.

"We talked about you, mostly. Feathers came with us as far as the newsagents."

Josh felt a stab of alarm. "You didn't tell them?"

"I told Lucy – I mean she's one of us."

"Yea."

"And she had some good ideas. We both did."

He didn't like the sound of that - good ideas about his own future. He looked at Megs' upright shoulders, shimmying ahead of him, and yawned. He couldn't cope with all this energy so soon after waking up. Megs had come on a lot in the last year. She seemed to know where she was going. He wished he felt the same. He plodded along behind her, locked in his own thoughts.

He noticed that they had already reached the harbour. "Where are we heading now?" he asked.

Megs didn't seem to hear him. "Oh, by the way, I met Sharon in town this morning," she said in a neutral sort of voice.

"Oh, yes?"

"Yes. She asked, 'how's Josh?' and she gave one of her tinkly, little laughs. I think she sounded nervous."

"And what did you say?".

"I said you were fine. I thought she looked surprised. I mean pleased, but surprised."

That didn't sound right. He thought about those motor bikes revving up outside the party. They obviously knew he was there. Could she have known something? "She wouldn't do that sort of thing," he said aloud.

"Do what?" Megs turned to let him catch up.

"She wouldn't have talked to those bikers. Maybe she heard something from one of her friends."

"Or her brother."

"I didn't know she had a brother. How do you know all this, Megs?"

"She's in my class, remember? She's a bit of a teacher's pet. She did mention having an older brother who was a bit of a hard man. I didn't take any notice – I thought she was just trying to get in with the cool crowd."

"Are you one of the cool crowd, Megs?" Josh teased her.

"I'm not in any crowd," said Megs. "There's one or two girls who are okay. Seriously, Josh, I think we have to check this brother out. He has his own gang. 'The Wild Gang' – that's what they're called. His dad's name is Bill. I thought we should call on him and see what his son's got to say. You may even recognise him."

Josh thought of the man with the brawny arms who'd half strangled him the night before. So that was Sharon's dad!

They had passed the harbour now and started past the docks and derelict estates that led to Mile End Road. He kept thinking about Sharon, knowing about the attack. She had to have known! That was why she had invited him to the party, not just because she fancied him. His eyes filled with disappointment and shame. He tried to shake off his foul mood before Megs turned round and noticed.

The street had a more friendly air in the daylight. Two kids kicked a football around, using dustbins as makeshift goal posts, and people stood in doorways or called across to each other from upstairs windows. Josh found the house he was looking for with ease because he remembered that he had only broken one window on that side of the street. Besides, he recognised some of the neighbours. "It's the young Guardian!" cried one of them. "And the girl's with him!" cried the owner of that shrill voice. More windows opened up and down the street. The man with the brawny arms appeared in his doorway and welcomed them into his snug sitting room.

Sharon's dad was a handsome, big-boned man. He wore a well-ironed, open-neck yellow shirt and smelt of aftershave. He greeted Josh in a friendly but forceful manner. "Josh, my boy," he said. "Come in! And Megs too. You're Megs, right? You're the one that phoned me this morning, right?"

Josh was surprised not to see Sharon there. He had a blurred memory of the tall youth dangling by the window. He'd been the one who laughed when his leader spoke and followed him down the street. He looked about eighteen, going on thirty, and had a thin pock-marked face. He wore a black biker's jacket with the words 'The Wild Gang' picked out on one side.

"You recognise this lad?" his dad asked him, pointing to Josh.

"I dunno."

His dad grabbed his son and pushed him into a chair. "What kind of answer's that?" he asked. "Where were you last night?"

"I took Sharon to the party, didn't I?"

"And then what?"

"We met this bloke, and he asked if Josh was at the party, and I said 'yea' because that's what Sharon told me."

Megs gave Josh a nudge, and he asked, "This guy you met, did he have the letters 'RR' on his jacket?"

Jason stared at him. "That's the one, yea."

"So you helped him find Josh," said Jason's father, glaring down at his son. "What happened when you found him?"

"Nothing, he just took his phone and then we chased him down this street."

"So, he stole his phone?"

"He didn't steal it, honest! He just broke it and threw it away."

His dad wiped the hair back from his face and stared hard at his son. "So why would he do that? Didn't you find it strange when he did that?"

"I dunno. Them phones are expensive."

His dad raised his right arm in the air above his son's head, restraining the urge to hit him. "Didn't you think it a bit strange – I mean this wasn't just a mugging - this was more than a mugging – didn't that cross your mind?"

Jason nodded. "Yea, I thought that was a bit odd."

"So, you were going to chase this lad down to the docks. What then?"

"I dunno what then, do I? We never went to the docks."

"Where did your friend go after that?" asked Josh. "Did he tell you where he lived?"

Jason stared at him.

His dad raised his arm again. "You heard him. Where did he go?"

"I told you. I didn't know him. Better ask Sharon. He went off, that's all..."

His dad turned away from his son in disgust. "I think that's all the sense you're going to get out of this lad," he said, as they parted company. "Leastways, this bloke you mentioned is not from round here. He may not even be from Amaryllis. It's police protection you need."

Josh and Megs left the house and climbed the sacred path which wound up the mountain towards the Temple of Harmony. They'd reached the first of 'The Nine Stages of Contemplation' - a paved area with a few kiosks and an open-air cafe called 'Pilgrims' Rest'. *A nice place*, thought Josh, to sit and contemplate being hunted down by a biker with RR printed on his jacket.

"Are you going to tell Feathers?" Megs asked.

Josh gazed down the slope at the pirate ships with crimson sails anchored in the glittering bay. Where before he'd seen excitement and beauty, he saw only hopelessness. "I suppose I'll have to," he said. "Feathers will tell the police and it won't do any good. There must be plenty of people out there willing to kill for money."

Megs sat sipping lemonade through a straw, watching him. The sunlight reflected on her long, black hair. *How did she manage to look so cool?* He thought again about Sharon. He looked up and blushed when he realised that Megs was still speaking.

"You're still the Guardian," she said, placing her glass on the table.

"Yea, it's weird being hunted down for something you only half believe in."

"What! You don't believe in being Guardian?"

"I don't think it's important now. I've surrendered the Guardian's necklace, which everyone agreed was a good thing, because it meant we could all live together in peace. So I don't have visions anymore and – best of all – I don't have epileptic fits. I can't see why the Prince is so keen to get rid of me."

"You still believe in what the Guardian stands for," Megs insisted, pulling him to his feet.

"Yea," he agreed, half-heartedly, following her down the steps. "I believe in love and cooperation and the Temple of Harmony and all that stuff. The idea of having a Guardian used to be what kept us from fighting. But that's not true anymore. So, I can't understand why the Prince still wants to kill me."

They'd reached the bottom of the steps now and Josh hurried after Megs along the avenue towards the old part of town. "Hang on, Megs," he called out. "Where are you going?"

"To see Sharon, remember? You'd like that, wouldn't you?"

"But she doesn't live here!"

"No, but she works here on weekends. 'The Lucky Luke' – it's a café."

She led Josh across the road into a corner café with four empty tables. Sharon sat behind the counter, flicking through the pages of a magazine. She had long bleach-blonde hair, a pale, pretty face and pouting lips. She smiled when she saw Josh and straightened up, brushing her hair away from her eyes. "Hi, Josh," she said. "I wasn't expecting you."

At that moment, she saw Megs, and the shy twinkle went out of her eyes. "Hi, Megs," she said and looked from one to the other. "What's up?"

"I've brought your lover-boy to see you," said Megs. "'Better ask Sharon'. That's what your brother said. So that's what we've come to do – ask you."

Sharon's eyes widened. "Ask me what? I don't know what you're talking about." She slipped round the counter and took a cloth to one of the tables. "Look, it'll get busy soon," she called over her shoulder. "If that's all you came for, I can't help. Sorry."

Josh went over to the table that Sharon was cleaning. "Look, Sharon," he said, "You invited me to that party and a bloke nearly killed me. You really have to help me."

Her eyes looked troubled. "I'm sorry about that," she said in a quiet voice. "I never thought that guy meant to harm you. Just meet you. That was all."

"You knew him."

"Never!"

"At least your brother knew him. And you must have seen him around – a guy in a black leather jacket, remember?"

She nodded. "He comes in here sometimes. Asked if I knew you; that's all. I must have said something about the party. That's all. I swear!"

"Do you know where he's staying?"

She looked at the stairway behind the counter as if she was scared of something. "Up there," she said. "The boss has a spare room, which he lets out sometimes. You won't tell him I told you? Please!"

Josh put an arm round her shoulder. "Come on, Sharon! You have to help us!" he said. "We have to tell the police. We need you as evidence."

Sharon started to cry; tears of anger and frustration mingled with eye liner and formed black streaks down her cheeks. "I just done what my brother asked me," she said. "I didn't know they meant to harm you."

Josh felt sad at the thought of having trusted her. "Sorry, Sharon," he said. "We really have to trace that man before he makes another attempt to kill me."

"For goodness' sake!" cried Megs. "Stop soft-soaping her! She's got to come with us. She caused all this trouble in the first place!"

Sharon nodded and wiped away her tears. She scribbled a message for her boss and meekly followed them out of the café.

# CHAPTER THREE

B y the time the police had taken statements and cautioned Sharon's boss for harbouring a known criminal, Josh and Megs realised they were in for a late night and Feathers needed to be told. The old man stumped into the police station shortly after midnight to collect them and drive them home.

Josh sat beside Megs on the sofa and watched while Feathers made himself comfortable in the big armchair. They waited while he rubbed his eyes and scratched his beard and helped himself to a large glass of wine. Finally, he coughed and gave them a long, hard look, and thanked them for making his life interesting.

Josh glanced at Megs and tried not to smile.

Then Feathers took another sip of wine and said he wouldn't mind it for the next few days if the interest factor could be reduced. In fact, he wouldn't mind a bit of boredom and routine, like having meals at regular times and locking up the house at midnight, sure that all the occupants were in bed and not somewhere in the town being chased by a hired assassin. At this point, he wished them good night and stumbled upstairs to bed.

Josh spent an anxious night wondering what Feathers would say the next morning. As they all gathered in the kitchen for a late breakfast, Josh glanced across at Megs, who nodded and then launched into his speech.

"Look, I'm very sorry about last night," he said, "and the night before. I'll be more careful next time. We both will. But please don't tell my parents! They'll go crazy. And they'll either call us home or ask for police protection and it won't do any good because the Prince wants to kill me. And he'll succeed unless I have my hands free to fight back... somehow."

Feathers listened carefully and nodded. "You have a point, young Josh," he said. "At least, you had until you got to the somehow bit. That's the bit that interests me – the somehow. Have you ever wondered why the Prince is so set on killing you?"

"Well, we know that!" said Megs. "Josh's the Guardian."

Feathers shook his head. "That's got something to do with it, no doubt. But there's got to be something else he's afraid of. Maybe you know something about him that he wants hidden; something about his past, perhaps, that would destroy his reputation among his core supporters?"

Josh recalled his one and only meeting with the Prince in his bungalow on Windfree. "How could I know anything?" he asked. "I only met him once – and just for a few minutes."

"Maybe you learned something about him you weren't supposed to know. Do you think he is sincere, for example?"

Josh thought of the young man he met in that humble cottage in the hills of Windfree. He remembered his eyes that glistened with sincerity, as he revealed his sincere intention of driving the colonists out of the Western Isles. Then he remembered what he hadn't been meant to see behind the closed door of the Prince's sitting room; the vast cavern occupied by soldiers and secretaries and modern weapons of war. And he remembered some of those soldiers, with circlets round their necks, which transmitted pain and pleasure at the Prince's command.

"I learned that he's sincere but mad, and also cruel and a bit of a fraud!"

"Well, maybe that's it," Feathers decided. "Deep down, he's a fraud, and he knows it. There's something not quite right about him; something he doesn't want his supporters to know."

Josh exchanged glances with Megs. "Feathers," he asked, "does that mean we can stay?"

Feathers grunted. "Did I ever say you couldn't?" he asked. "Amaryllis is about the safest place for you at the moment and Megs here seems to be giving you better protection than the police can provide." He gave a short laugh. "And it may not have occurred to you, but I actually like having you here! It enlivens my dreary routine, having you young people around, staying out late, and getting chased by assassins. It reminds me of all the adventures I used to have in my youth."

"Thanks, Feathers."

"My pleasure. What are you looking for, Megs?"

"Do you have a copy of the Piratica, Feathers?"

"Over there, on the top shelf somewhere. But the only bit that will interest you is this little fragment from the book of prophecies. I made a copy of the page because I thought it might tell us something. It's the only page that refers to recent times."

He unfolded the page and read the words in a slow, clear voice.

*When the King is killed*
*And the mist is lifted,*
*There will come a time*
*Of great forgetting.*

*Red flowers will grow*
*In every land,*
*And the Rebel Prince*
*Will deceive the unwitting.*


*The necklace*
*Of the Guardian Queen*
*Must be restored*
*To its ancient setting.*


"It doesn't tell us anything at all," complained Josh. "The King must be Machin – he's dead now- and we know the Prince is profiting from the dodgy medical trade. The fields of Windfree are full of those red oblivion flowers. I've seen them! And we did restore the necklace!"

"I think it's amazing how they managed to prophesy all that!" said Megs. "And what about 'deceive the unwitting.'? That's new, isn't it? It's saying he's got something to hide."

"If you want to hear something even more amazing," said Feathers, rising to his feet, "we can consult the oracle! That's where the book of Prophesies gets printed. It's up near the temple. Who knows? They may be able to tell us more than you'll find in that book. Do you two feel like a short walk?"

Josh groaned inwardly. He remembered exactly how long that walk would be and doubted whether they'd learn anything new at the end of it. But Megs had already grabbed Feathers' hand and was pulling him towards the door, and he knew it would be unwise to express his doubts.

The climb up the mountainside in the searing heat took more than an hour. Feathers refused to stop for a drink, but sweat poured down his reddening face by the time they reached the last step. Flies settled on his cheeks, and he began to huff and puff and brush them away and complain that oracles were a waste of time, and he couldn't imagine what idiot had suggested the visit in the first place. Josh grinned and ran off to fetch him a drink of water while Megs searched out a stone seat in a shady spot outside the ancient library. When Josh returned, the old man seized the bottle, took a long draught, wiped his mouth, and poured the remains of the cold liquid over his mostly bald head.

The Oracular Department occupied the top floor of the library, which turned out to be a spacious, modern building a few steps up the mountain from the Temple of Harmony. As soon as Josh stepped out of the lift on the second floor behind Feathers and Megs, he could hear the printing presses banging out copies of the Piratica behind the wall to his left. To his right, beyond the reception area, several piratical secretaries in smart white shirts and red neckties sat at computers in separate cubicles along one glass-fronted wing of the building overlooking the woods.

Feathers led the way to the reception desk where a young piratical secretary stood up to greet them. "You're Josh, aren't you?" she said, "the young Guardian? And you must be Megs. So, this gentleman must be the famous explorer, Sir William Feathers. How can I help you?"

Feathers lumbered forward, smiling broadly. "We've come to consult the Oracle," he said.

She raised the flap on the counter to let them through. "Well, for the moment, that's me, as I'm the only one free. Step into my office and I'll see what I can do for you."

She led them into the nearest glass cubicle and sat facing them across a desk, staring into a computer screen. "Josh Flagsmith, isn't it? You're mentioned in the prophetic books. Ah, here's the most recent bit:

*When the King is killed*
*And the mist is lifted—*

Josh looked over her shoulder. "These verses are old," he said. "The necklace has been restored. We know that!"

The secretary leaned forward across her desk. "You see, the prophesies are constantly evolving," she said. "They are never complete until the events they describe are over. That's why there's only one true version of the Piratica, which is the one being prepared next door."

"Then you can't call them prophesies!" Megs protested.

The secretary smiled. "We call them post-prophesies," she explained. "I can arrange for you to see the revised version of the passage relating to Josh if you like."

"But if you can change it whenever you want, what's the point?" asked Megs, her face flushed with disappointment.

The secretary nodded. "I understand how you feel, Megs. The art of divination isn't perfect."

"Well, it certainly isn't future!" muttered Feathers.

"Nonetheless," the secretary continued, choosing to ignore this remark. "My oracular department has discovered a recent addition to the prophetic text, which may be of use to you. I am not allowed to let a copy leave this building, but I can read it to you, if you like:

*But pirates flocked*
*To the Prince's cause,*
*All harmony*
*And peace forgetting*

*Until they found*
*His secret flaw*

*There seemed no end*
*To such blood-letting.*

You must discover the Prince's weakness," said the lady, leading them downstairs to the exit. "I wish you good luck with your quest."

"That was about as much use as visiting Sybil the sybil," said Josh, as they wandered down the steps.

To his surprise, Megs disagreed. "We did learn something," she said. "Maybe two things. The Prince has a weakness."

"And what's the second thing?"

"He must know what you are trying to find out. Otherwise, why is he trying to kill you? I wonder if the Prince knew we were going to visit the Oracle."

"I don't know. I suppose we were bound to at some point."

"Then that's probably an added reason why he tried to have you killed. He knew we would visit the oracle, and he's afraid of what we might learn."

"Which is nothing," said Feathers.

Josh shook his head. "Hang on, Feathers. Megs is right. The Prince has a weakness, just as you said, and it must be something related to his past, something which would destroy his credibility if people ever got to know about it."

"That's easy then," said Feathers. "The most likely assumption is that he isn't who he claims to be – but I've no idea why Josh is in a special position to know that." He stopped and took a rolled-up newspaper out of his trouser pocket and waved it like a baton before their eyes. "I picked this up from the desk while you were talking to that strange man," he said, brandishing it. "Look, there's a café round the corner. Let's stop and have a drink. It's been a hot day and, besides, I want to show you some bad news."

Feathers led the way to a table in the far corner of the café, protected by the over-arching shade of a walnut tree.

"That's the Amaryllis Gazette," he said, handing the open newspaper to Josh. "That biker of yours is dead. Look, there's a picture of him. They found him on a garbage tip somewhere on the outskirts of town, stabbed in several places."

"Why would he have him killed?" asked Josh. "Do you think he knew something?"

"I doubt it," said Feathers. "He failed to kill you. 'Fail and you're dead'; that's the message. Which means he's already selected another assassin. So you'd better watch your step!" He accepted the newspaper back from Josh and turned to an inside page. "However, there's another item here which is not headline news in Amaryllis, but which worries me almost as much. The Prince has set fire to all the gunge plantations on Humphrey's island and Windfree."

Josh thought about that time he'd met the Prince in Windfree. "He said he wanted to do that," he murmured, "but I never thought he was serious. What does it mean?"

"Not much as far as Amaryllis is concerned," said Feathers, "because people here grow their own food, but for islands like Colony Island and Crown Colony, it spells disaster. The whole fast-food industry depends on those gunge bushes."

Josh thought about the other plans the Prince had mentioned. It had seemed like a game the way he'd talked about them at the time. Perhaps it was a game to the Prince. But if he really meant to drive out the colonists from the islands where they settled nearly four hundred years ago, the war would spread throughout the Western Isles.

The old man shook his head. "We should have seen this coming," he said. "The Prince has got us all by the throat!" He folded the paper up and stuffed it in his jacket. Then he rubbed his eyes and said, "We have to find his weakness. Don't ask me how. From where I'm sitting, he looks pretty strong to me."

Josh had never seen the old man at such a loss. "Feathers," he began.

"Yes, young Josh?"

"You knew the Prince, didn't you?"

"Briefly, in his younger days, yes. My son knew him better, of course. He was in the same class at school."

"Where's your son now?"

Feathers had a twinkle in his eye again. He sat up and thumped his knee with his great fist. "That's an idea! Bless me! Why didn't I think of it? He's a teacher now at the school where he was once a pupil. I'd love to see him again before I die. That's what we must do, my boy; go to Crown Colony and check out what he can tell us!"

## Chapter Four

Their plane, packed with cheering colonist football supporters returning from Amaryllis, touched down on Elephantia in the late afternoon. The air stewardess led them through an arched entrance in a huge white circular building, which rose straight in the air and then, halfway up, curved inwards into a dome.

Josh had never seen anything built on such a colossal scale before. He gazed up at the dome of tinted glass, held in place by steel supports which met at the apex fifty yards above his head.

When he stepped inside, he could see that each separate section was walled off, but the walls only reached halfway up the building so that you could always see the domed roof and the sun or the stars shining through.

Feathers shepherded Josh and Megs to the end of the queue, proceeding through passport control. Josh noticed how energised Feathers had become at the thought of seeing his son again.

Megs grabbed his hand. "People are looking at us," she whispered. "Some of them know who we are." Her eyes shifted to Feathers, ahead of them in the queue, still chatting with a pirate family and their small son. "Do you think we should warn him?" she asked. "I mean, some of the people in this queue may be fans of the Prince."

"Hardly," he said with a smile. "Just listen to this lot!"

A group of colonist football supporters in front of them had just broken into song.

Before they got to the punchline, a massive clap of thunder from high up above pitched his mind into utter blackness. He ducked and covered his head, squeezing his eyes shut as he heard the crash and rumble of falling masonry and the tinkle of shattering glass. The rumbling went on and on. When he finally opened his eyes, he saw that all normal activity had stopped. Everyone in the queue stood staring up at a jagged hole in the dome, directly over the Arrivals Hall beyond the wall in front of them. He could hear the muffled shouts and screams of his shocked and wounded fellow passengers on the other side of the wall.

Josh felt shocked and awed. Bombing an airport in the capital city of the largest and most powerful island in the Western Isles made him realise for the first time the full scale of the Prince's power and ambitions. He turned and grabbed hold of Megs, who had made a move towards the door that led to the Arrivals Hall.

"Don't Megs!" he whispered. "It's not safe yet. Look up at the roof! There's more to come down yet."

As he spoke, one of the steel struts came loose from its moorings, dangled in the air a bit, then came crashing down, bringing with it part of the glass framework and the masonry that formed its base. Megs turned her tear-stained face towards him, seeking his advice. "Those poor people!" she whispered. "We've got to go and help them! I can hear mothers with babies in there – the ones they let through first. I can hear those babies crying."

Josh kept his arm around her and felt her chest heave as she sobbed. He wished he could express his feelings with the same immediacy. His mind was always at work, thinking, *who did this?*, *what's next?* and, *what's the best way to help?* He looked at his fellow passengers, who all stood dumbstruck like himself, staring up at the dome and listening to the shrieks and groans of the victims down below.

Then the noise died down, and Josh could hear the calmer voices of officials attending to the casualties, and directing the passengers who'd escaped the blast out of the hall. Soon these sounds were drowned out by the insistent high-pitched sirens of ambulances and police cars racing to the scene. Then even these sounds gave way to the voices all around him, as the people on his side of the wall came to terms with what had just happened and realised that it might easily have happened to themselves.

He looked around for Feathers, but couldn't find him anywhere in the queue. A lady standing behind him asked, "Looking for granddad, love? He's gone to the toilet."

He nodded and thanked her. "One of the staff escorted him," the lady added. "I think he was feeling a bit sick after what just happened."

Josh knew in a flash that couldn't be right. He saw the toilets signed up above the passageway on his left. Feathers didn't need an escort. He just thanked the lady, grabbed Megs' hand, and headed for the passageway.

He didn't go far. At that moment, he saw Feathers emerging from the toilet, mopping his brow, and staring uncertainly around him. He gave Josh a feeble wave of the hand and walked with heavy steps towards him like a man in a dream. "I've just seen a ghost," he said. "Ronald Fleck – you remember him?!"

"Fleck's dead!" protested Megs.

"I wish that were true. He didn't die in that aircraft as we all imagined. It was the pilot that died. Fleck shot him and flew away. He really enjoyed telling me about that. He's been working with the

Prince all along. It was Fleck that guided that plane towards the airport and told him when to drop his bomb."

"What did he want?" asked Josh.

"He wanted to give you a message. The Prince doesn't want to kill you. Killing the Guardian would not be a popular move, but he'll do it if you keep digging around into his guilty secrets."

Josh stumbled for words. "So all those people who died..." he began.

Feathers placed a heavy arm on his shoulder. "They'd have died anyway," he said. "Bombing the airport had always been the plan. If Fleck hadn't spotted you at the back of the queue, the entire roof would have collapsed and they'd have tried to kill us all."

"Where is he now?" asked Megs.

"I've no idea. I nearly had him, but he sprayed something in my eyes and slipped away. I wish I'd managed to throttle him. The world would be a better place without him. Look at all the unnecessary destruction he's caused. This was just a part of it." He pointed towards the door of the Arrivals Hall, where some of the passengers who didn't require ambulances were slowly returning.

First among them was an elderly lady with a little girl slung over her shoulder. The girl was sobbing uncontrollably. "I'm her granny," she explained to them. "Both her parents died in the explosion."

"Let me hold her," said Megs, "while you get some first aid. I was the same age when my parents died. Believe me, I know how it feels."

The lady seemed happy to leave the child with Megs, while Josh led her to get her wounds seen to in the first aid room. "Her name's Alice," she said over her shoulder. "My husband and I live not far from here. We'll try and make a good home for her."

Josh noticed how the little girl settled in Megs' arms. Megs stroked her hair and whispered calming words into her ear. Later, when he returned with the lady, washed and bandaged, from the first aid room, Megs smiled and passed her the sleeping bundle in her arms. The lady whispered her thanks and departed.

The first aid room had been busy. Most of the passengers with minor injuries from the carnage in the Arrivals Hall had been bandaged up and left, and the queue in the Passport Hall sprang to life as the passengers turned to each other and shared their shock and horror at the wanton massacre they had just witnessed. Josh didn't hear anybody in that crowd who wouldn't have been glad to strangle the Prince. *So, what was the point of it all?* he wondered.

Shortly afterwards, a stewardess appeared at the entrance to the airport and held up a hand to halt the rush of fellow passengers towards her. "I'll deal with you all in a moment," she said. "First, I want to call through any passengers on a transit flight to Crown Colony."

Feathers raised his hand. "That's us," he whispered. "We seem to be the only ones."

"There should be eight of you," said the stewardess, as they boarded the coach. "The driver will have to stop outside the Arrivals Halls to pick up any of your fellow passengers who are in a fit state to join you."

Five football supporters climbed on board the coach outside the Arrivals Hall. "We're among the lucky ones," said their spokesman, a big man still wearing his team colours. "It's still chaos in there, I can tell you."

"Were there many casualties?" asked Feathers.

"Twenty dead at the moment, but some of the ones we saw carried away on stretchers looked in a bad way. I tell you, it's almost as bad here as it is in Crown Colony. Enjoy your journey, fellows."

He lumbered past to join his mates at the back of the coach.

# CHAPTER FIVE

J osh sat at the front with Feathers and Megs. He stared through the window and tried to focus on his surroundings. But the memory of what he'd seen and heard at the airport kept interfering with his thoughts.

He shook his head and gazed out of the window. He'd never been to Elephantia before. The airport they'd just left was situated close to the harbour, and it took them nearly an hour to navigate the busy streets of Newport, the capital. It appeared to be twice as big as Paradise City, the capital of Crown Colony, which was the largest city he'd ever visited. The coach driver had to weave his way through the narrow streets of the old town surrounding the harbour, then through the high-rise buildings of the commercial centre, crammed with shoppers and office workers, and then on through the endless suburbs.

They didn't talk much on the coach either. Feathers asked several times if they were all right, but beyond that, they couldn't find much to say. Josh knew that Feathers had been through many near-death experiences in his long, adventurous life, but for him and Megs, what happened at the airport was a life-changing event. He put an arm over Megs' shoulder. She gave him a sad smile and let him leave it there.

He thought of the way she'd cradled that girl at the airport. "I'm glad you were there," he said, gently releasing his arm.

"What do you mean?" she asked, looking up at him with a quizzical grin. "I'm always there."

"I know, but... this was different."

Up to now, he'd thought of the Prince as a lonely fanatic, with a small band of followers camped on the poor island of Windfree. He knew he had a network of soldiers and spies and assassins capable of creating random attacks on isolated individuals. But he had never imagined that the Prince could muster up the military might to threaten the largest island in the Western Isles. That bomb could easily have landed on them. But it hadn't. And now he knew that the Prince had planned that too. He wanted him alive because it was bad for morale to kill the Pirate Guardian, but he'd kill him anyway if he went on probing into his past. What could he have done? Josh wondered, that was worse than killing a crowd of innocent passengers at an airport.

He followed Feathers and Megs as they hurried off the coach and carried their bags through to the departure lounge of the much smaller Newfields Airport. After passing through passport control, they found the other passengers already seated in rows in the departure hall, watching the news on the telescreen. Earnest and windswept, the reporter stood in front of a glass-fronted building. The view widened to show ambulances and police cars parked outside the entrance and people streaming out of the main doors. Josh and Megs looked at one another. Was this the scene they had just witnessed at Newport?

But the announcer wasn't speaking about Elephantia! "A bomb has been found in the arrivals hall of Crown Colony airport," he said. "Experts are defusing it as I speak." He paused. "So far," he said, "nobody has claimed responsibility for this bomb, but we can safely assume that the source is somewhere on Humphrey's Island or Windfree. If, as many people suggest, this is the work of a man calling himself the 'Rebel Prince,' it is highly likely that the war will be extended to Humphrey's Island too. The Parliament of Crown Colony is holding an emergency session as I speak." At that moment, the screen went blank, and an official walked in to announce that flights to Crown Colony would resume the following morning.

All around the lounge, Josh could hear people talking about the bomb and the Rebel Prince. He noticed that the people around him were all colonists. The seats on the other side of the aisle were all occupied by pirates. "Am I allowed to sit here?" he asked the grey-haired lady sitting next to him.

She gave him a friendly smile and asked, "Why ever not?" She put aside the book she was reading and peered at him over his spectacles. Then she looked around her and said, "Oh. I see what you mean! It never used to be like that on our island. Pirates and colonists have always got along well here. It's these recent terrorist attacks that have driven us apart, not that the locals have got much to do with all that."

"Have there been many attacks?" asked Megs.

The lady searched in her large leather handbag and pulled out a newspaper. "Funny you should ask!" she said. "I've just been reading about that. Since the attacks started nearly a year ago, there have been more than fifty bomb attacks reported in Elephantia. Most of them have been attacks on individuals. Bombing airports is a new development."

"Were the bombers wearing circlets?"

She gave them a searching look and exclaimed. "Oh! You know about those wretched circlets? Yes, I think in most cases they wore circlets. So, you could say that they didn't have much choice. It's the power behind all this that frightens me." She sighed and patted his hand. "Well, it's still a lovely island, Elephantia, though it's best to avoid the main town at the moment. I live in the country where food is plentiful, and pirates and colonists get along together as they always have done."

She pointed at a poster of a youngish, broad-shouldered man in a green polo-neck sweater and black jeans. Josh thought he could have been a sportsman of some kind. Underneath the poster lay the caption: "Vote for Jack Sands. Let's get our island moving again!"

"That's the man I'll be voting for," she said. "He wants to put the island on a war footing, uniting pirates and colonists in a common cause. He aims to take the fight to the enemy and rediscover our strength before that Prince walks all over us."

They went silent as the news programme resumed. The reporter was back in the studio now. He referred to his notes. "Over in Colony Island, Magnus Maxtrader has announced that two of his halls of pings will shortly be converted into gardening centres to cater for the increased demand for home-grown food."

"Pure propaganda," whispered Feathers. "They're just about to start a second war they can't win and soon they're going to run out of food. At the moment, the Prince holds all the cards."

The attendant returned to announce that the flight would depart the following morning at 10 a.m. and the hospitality section was open for passengers needing overnight accommodation. Josh walked in a dream behind Josh and Megs, thinking about the Prince and his supposed weakness, and wondering if any weakness would be enough to topple him from his winning ways.

# CHAPTER SIX

They arrived in Crown Colony around lunchtime on the following morning and booked into Fairways Hotel not far from Portlands College where Feathers' son taught Piratican – the ancient language and culture of the pirate world. From his bedroom window, Josh could see kids in black shorts and red and white striped shirts, playing separate football matches on acres of green fields.

Despite its good view of the harbour, a short walk from the centre of town, the small hotel had only one other guest; a travelling salesman from Windfree. "We're luckier than some," said the manager, emerging from the kitchen and coming to sit at their table. "We have a large garden, so we're able to grow some of our own food. The problem is the bees."

Feathers raised his eyebrows. "You mean you can't get any honey?" he asked.

The manager laughed. "Honey would be nice," he said, moistening his lips. "But we don't get much fruit either. Bees are needed to pollinate." He reached into his pocket and placed what looked like a small insect in the palm of his hand. "Here! Take a look at this!"

"It's a dead bee," said Megs. "Do you mean the bees are dying off, all of a sudden?"

"Take a closer look," said the manager. "You can hold it in your hand if you like."

"Poor thing!" said Megs, stroking it with her finger. "Its wings are a bit stiff."

"What do you think they are made of?" asked the manager, smiling.

Megs shrugged. "Well, it feels like plastic," she said.

"And what if I tell you it is plastic?" he asked, searching her eyes for understanding.

"Then it's not a real bee!"

The manager put the insect back into his pocket. "It's a miniature drone," he explained.

"Maxtrader is manufacturing thousands of these little toys. You have to guide them, of course, like model airplanes, but it's a bit tricky getting them to settle on a flower. The modern ones are more sophisticated, but the device has never really caught on. Mind you, there are other insects capable of pollinating flowers. Most of the farmers round here think the same."

He stood up and said, "Still, lack of fresh fruit is not our main problem. It's lack of guests. The longer this war goes on, the more hotels will have to close down." He mopped his brow. "Waiting for your son, are you?" he asked Feathers. "Teaches at Portlands, I believe? Good school that! I'd send my own son there, if I could afford the fees."

Josh had no problem identifying the large man stooping in the doorway. He looked as his father might have done forty years ago if he'd been a schoolteacher instead of an explorer. He had long, shaggy hair and glasses and a short, straggly beard. His blue eyes were friendly and placid – they lacked the fire and sparkle of his dad's. He was as broad as his father and almost a head taller. Father and son embraced, and tears formed at the corners of Feathers' eyes. "This is Geoffrey," he said, "It's a whole year since I last saw him."

"A year and a bit," agreed Geoffrey.

"Is it as long as that?" asked Feathers. He looked up at the broad, smiling face looming above him. "Thank goodness you haven't grown any taller. Otherwise, I'd need to stand on a chair. Let me introduce you to my two charges!"

Geoffrey blinked and extended a huge hand to greet them.

Josh pointed out of the window.

"Are those your kids in the red and white stripes?" he asked. "I've been watching them playing football."

"Geoffrey used to be good at that sport," said Feathers. "What position did you play in, Geoffrey?"

Geoffrey laughed. "Goalie. Because of my height, I suppose. Well, probably my width came into it too."

"Was the Prince in your team?"

"Which one? We had several princes in those days."

"He means Rupert," explained his father, "the man who calls himself the Rebel Prince."

"Oh, Rupert!" He turned to Josh and Megs. "Yes, let's get the business of the day over with first. I understand from my father that he's the reason for your visit. I don't know how much I can tell you. He wasn't a Prince, and he wasn't called Rupert in those days – not when I first knew him. He was called Richard – Rupert was his middle name." Geoffrey turned to his father. "Look, we've got lots to talk about. I'll show these young people around and I'll be right back. Mr Sims is expecting them."

Feathers nodded and settled himself in an armchair facing the garden. "You'll have dinner with us, of course?" he asked.

"Of course! And tomorrow's a holiday. We've got lots of time. I'll be back in an hour."

Josh lagged behind and let Megs do the talking. He wanted to keep a lookout for dangers lurking unseen.

"Was Rupert a friend of yours?" Megs asked, hurrying along beside Geoffrey as he led them up the lane that led to the school grounds.

Geoffrey bent his head to reply. "Yes. We were both new boys, and we stuck up for each other when the other kids tried to bully us." He laughed. "Well, they didn't bully me so much because of my size. Rupert had a hard time because he was a pirate – or, said he was – most of our lot were clean-living colonists."

"What do you mean by 'said he was'?" Josh called out.

Geoffrey stopped in his stride. "Well, he started to make an issue of it," he said. "Something must have happened to him during the first summer holidays. He came back talking a lot of nonsense about being descended from the Rebel Prince. That's when he changed his name to Rupert. Then the bullying got worse, and his parents took him away. I think they sent him to Amaryllis after that."

*Amaryllis!* thought Josh. He'd have to do some digging around when he got back.

They wandered through the school gates and followed Geoffrey down a gravel path towards an imposing stone structure hung with ivy and wisteria. He pointed down a dark corridor to the right. "That's the way to the staff room," he said. "School finished an hour ago and the kids are back in their boarding houses or outside, playing games. It's not as quiet as this during class times, I can tell you!"

He led them into a large, panelled room with cupboards, notices and scribbled memos on the walls and a table at one end, covered with books, papers, half-empty coffee cups and cardboard boxes full of pens, pencils, scissors and chalk. At the other end of the room, two young teachers bent over a game of snooker. "Is Sims around?" Geoffrey asked them.

"He'll be back in a moment," one of them answered, head poised over his cue.

"Sims is the man we need to see," Geoffrey whispered. "He was around in Rupert's day. He used to teach history. Still does. He's expecting you, so he should be here soon."

A bald man in a worn green jacket exploded into the room and introduced himself as Mr Sims. He had a wispy white moustache and watery blue eyes. He shook Josh's hand up and down several times and did the same to Megs. "Come on, then!" he said in a cheery voice. "Where shall we sit? Over here in this corner. That do for you? Never mind about young Geoffrey! He can fend for himself. He's old enough." He gave a short, barking laugh. "Now, Josh, take the armchair. You can share it with your young lady. Take an arm each. That's right. No, it's not for me, thank you. If I sank into that chair, I doubt if I'd be able to get out. A hard chair with a straight back for me; that's right. Now where were we? Richard! Yes, nasty piece of work, Richard; always thought so. And I'm sure he knifed that boy, though we could never prove it. I've been doing some research before you came along. Just to refresh my memory. I've got it all up there." He pointed to one of the cupboards. "I'll get it down in a moment."

"Did you know his foster parents?" asked Josh.

Sims gave Josh a long, hard look. "I knew of them. I can't say I ever met them. I don't think the boy was ever very close to them. His nanny was the one who always took an interest in him. Nice lady. Still is."

"Do you mean she's still alive?" asked Josh.

The look on Sims' face prepared Josh for another explosion. Instead, Sims gave a short laugh. "Well, I'm alive, aren't I?" he said. "And I can tell you she's a good ten years younger than me." He looked round to see if the other staff members appreciated the joke.

"I'll introduce you to her if you like. She knew him from the day he was first adopted."

"So it's true then?" asked Megs. "He could be a pirate and he could be descended from the Prince!"

"He was certainly a pirate," said Sims, treating Megs to another of his hard looks. "I've no idea who his real father was, but I've got a copy of his adoption papers. That should tell us something." He pointed above his head. "Look, Geoffrey, you're taller than me. Would you mind having a look up there? It's right on top of all my other stuff – in a large red folder. Have you got it?"

Geoffrey peered into one of the marked lockers and retrieved a small plastic box. "Sorry, Sims," he said. "Apart from this, your locker's empty."

Sims let his mouth fall open. He looked fiercely round the room, like a dog that had just seen its food whipped away. "What do you mean 'empty'?" he asked. "Did you find the right locker?"

"Well, I found these." Geoffrey opened the box and held up a hard-boiled egg and a ham sandwich.

"Hm. Those are mine, I'm afraid." Sims cast his eyes around the room and grunted. "So, you definitely found the right locker." He looked angrily at the two teachers playing snooker. "You chaps!" he shouted. "Have you seen anyone touch my locker? No, of course, you haven't. Didn't think so! It took me a long time putting that folder together and bless me if one of the kids hasn't crept in and stolen it."

The idea of a schoolboy creeping into a staffroom to steal a folder struck Josh as far-fetched. A more sinister explanation clutched at his stomach. "What was in the folder?" he asked.

Sims reached in his jacket for a scrap of paper. "I made a list," he explained. He put on his glasses and studied it. "What's this?" he muttered. "Sometimes I can't read my own writing. A lettuce, two eggs, loaf of bread… no, that's my shopping list." He turned the paper over. "Ah, yes. Birth certificate. A copy of adoption papers. School reports. Police record. That relates to the incident that got him expelled."

"Expelled, was he?" asked Geoffrey, with an expression of surprise in his mild eyes. "I never knew that."

"Let's say his foster parents agreed to remove him," said Mr Sims. "They were worried enough at this stage to send him to a college in Amaryllis run on strict piratical lines– Saint Sophia's. Just what the boy needed!" He rubbed his bony hands and gave a short laugh.

Megs stood up and wandered across to the locker. She pushed a chair against the wall, climbed up and peered into the empty space. "It's quite dusty," she said. "What about finger- prints?"

Geoffrey and Sims exchanged glances. "I don't think we want the police involved at this stage," said Geoffrey. "I mean, it could all be a misunderstanding."

Josh noticed that the two young teachers had stopped their game and turned to listen.

"I don't think it was a misunderstanding," he said slowly. "Someone knew what was in that folder and stole it to stop us from finding something."

One of the two snooker players stepped forward. He turned and said, "Cheers, Douglas" to his colleague who was heading for the door, then pushed his floppy black hair away from his face and smiled at Josh and Megs. "My name's Jason," he said. "I don't like to say this," he added, looking at Sims, "but it has to be a teacher or, at least, someone that one of us knows. Who else was around when you mentioned the folder?"

"I don't know about that!" Sims exploded. "I was the soul of discretion!"

"Yes, of course, Mr Sims, but there must have been at least thirty teachers gathered in this room yesterday when the headmaster mentioned Josh's visit. And then, this morning, everyone saw you compiling your folder. You even dropped it on the floor at one point and I helped you put the papers back in order. Do you remember that?"

"I do remember that incident," said Sims, looking at the floor as if the papers still lay there. "So, what are you saying? Should we go to the police?"

To Josh's surprise, Megs nudged him and mouthed the word "no". She turned to Sims. "You mentioned a nanny," she said. "Do you think she knows the stuff you put in that folder?"

"Most of it."

"And could we see her?"

"Of course!"

"Then I think that's what we should do; best if we don't let on that we know the folder's been stolen yet."

She smiled at Sims, who got up and patted her on the shoulder. "Wise girl! Let's go there straightaway," he said. "I know where she lives- more or less-and it's not far. She's bound to be in at this time of day."

# CHAPTER SEVEN

T he nanny's apartment lay back the way they'd come, in a block of flats higher up the hill from the guesthouse. Sims pointed to the name 'Kelly Kelshaw' on the printed list of occupants attached to the wall beside the main entrance and led them up the steps to the second floor. He pressed the buzzer several times until a neighbour emerged from the door opposite. She was a large woman with a round face and yellow curly hair and she leant on a mop. "If you're looking for Marjory," she said, standing in the doorway and wiping her wet hands on her overalls, "she's at the hospital."

"Oh, she still works there, does she?" asked Sims.

The neighbour put away her mop and gave Sims a stare of surprise. "She gave that up ten years ago," she said. "No, she must have been taken ill. An ambulance came for her a few minutes ago. You just missed it."

Sims frowned. "Are you sure? I saw her cycling uphill the other day. That's more than I could do." He gave another of his barking laughs and turned to Geoffrey. "Sounds more like an accident."

"I don't know about that," the neighbour said. "I hope not. Poor Kelly! My son flooded the bathroom before he left for work, and I had to rush inside and mop up. Otherwise, I'd have taken more notice. All

I saw was a blue ambulance and two nurses lifting her into it on a stretcher. It came as a shock, but then, as I say, I was too busy to take it all in. I suppose she'll be at the hospital by now."

"That's it then," said Sims with a sigh. "We'd better go to the hospital. These young people are only here for a few days. They do need to see her. I only hope she's in a condition to speak to us."

Josh noticed that the door of the apartment stood slightly ajar. He bent down to inspect the lock. "Something's wrong here," he said, straightening up. "I think we should take a quick look inside."

Sims came over and tried the door himself. "Can't explain that," he said, shaking his head. "Well, I'm off to the hospital. I'll meet you there. I suppose they took her to the one down the hill."

"I suppose," the neighbour agreed. "Poor Kelly! I didn't know her well, but she looked fit enough – I'm sure it's nothing too serious." She turned to Sims. "Can I order you a taxi?"

Sims treated her to one of his sharp looks. "No thanks, I'll walk. It's not far." He waved an arm in the air and set off at a stiff stride down the hill.

Geoffrey looked at his watch and then at Josh and Megs. "My father must be wondering where we are," he said. "I think we should go to the hospital and then call it a day."

Josh felt Megs' arm on his shoulder. "Give us a moment," she said. "Something's wrong here. We need to check out that flat."

Geoffrey blinked. "Yes, well, no harm in having a quick look, I suppose," he said. "Do you think Miss Kelshaw would mind?" he asked the neighbour.

The neighbour shrugged. "Bless you!" she said. "I'm sure it won't do any harm so long as you don't move anything. She's a very tidy person. Not like me, I can assure you! And take your shoes off before you go in. She keeps her carpets spotless."

"Have you any idea what we're looking for?" asked Geoffrey, after they'd removed their shoes and entered the living room. "I mean, it's just as the lady says. Everything seems to be in perfect order."

Josh ignored him. He thought about the broken lock and the missing notes. He headed for the writing desk in the far corner of the room. "If nothing's been tampered with," he whispered to Megs, "the information we're looking for must be somewhere in here."

"There should be a photo of the Prince somewhere too," said Megs, peering above the mantelpiece. "I mean, if you looked after someone when he was a kid, surely you'd want to keep a photo of him somewhere?"

"The bedroom maybe?"

"I had a quick look. Nothing."

Geoffrey sat down heavily on the settee. "Well, you two seem to know what you're doing," he said. "I'll leave you to it." He yawned and picked up a magazine from the side table and started flicking through it.

"There's tons of stuff here!" Josh called out, on his hands and knees, examining the contents of the bottom drawer. "Mostly bills, I think, but I'd better check through it just in case. Have you found anything, Megs?"

"Just a minute."

Megs moved from the mantelpiece to switch off the electric fire. "That thing was burning my legs," she said. "Why would she leave the fire on when she went out?"

"She could have had a stroke or a heart attack," said Geoffrey.

"Yes, but in that case..."

Josh restored the bottom drawer to its frame and started on the second. It was hard to get this drawer open because it was stuffed with letters, postcards and old diaries – all neatly ordered according to date.

"That's strange!" Megs called out.

"What's strange, Megs?"

"There's loads of photos here, but none of the Prince. Unless..."
Her voice trailed away.

"Unless what?"

"There's a space above the mantelpiece where a framed photo once
hung. You can see the dust marks. There's no dust anywhere else. It
looks as if someone removed the photo recently. It wouldn't have been
Miss Kelshaw."

"How can you be so sure?" asked Geoffrey.

Megs sighed. "Look, Geoffrey, if you need to get back to your dad,
we quite understand. Josh and I will finish up here and then go on to
the hospital."

"I suppose I ought to be going," said Geoffrey, standing up and
looking at his watch. "My dad's expecting me, and I promised to drop
in on my girlfriend on my way home. You won't be long, I suppose?"

"I wonder what his girlfriend's like!" said Megs as he left the room.
"He seemed in a hurry to get away."

"Why do you say that?" asked Josh. He had already started on his
third drawer.

"It's obvious, isn't it? Someone's been in this room recently and
taken down that photo. He just didn't want to know."

Josh found the third drawer as cram full as the others. "There are
photos in this drawer too," he called out.

Megs wasn't listening. "I was trying to tell him something," she
said, "and he was looking at his watch. I hate it when people do that!
If Miss Kelshaw had removed that photo, she'd have got out her
duster straight away. There's not a speck of dust anywhere else in the
flat. Of course, you wouldn't know about these things, Josh!"

"I've done dusting before!"

"Yes, well....... have you found any photos of the Prince yet?"

"Not yet. At least, I don't think so. Quite a few photos of babies; I suppose one of them could be the Prince. They all look the same to me!"

"Apart from photos," asked Megs, "do you know what you expect to find?" She came and stood over him as he returned the third drawer to its frame.

"Hopefully, what's in here," he said as he stood up to open the top drawer; "his birth certificate for a start – the one that Simms copied. Here goes!" He pulled open the drawer.

"Oh!" said Megs.

"Yes, oh!" said Josh. "I think that clinches it! Why on earth would anyone cram three drawers full of letters and photos and stuff and leave the top drawer empty? That's where you put all the important stuff, isn't it? Come on! Let's go."

Megs stopped to stuff some objects into her shoulder bag and hurried after him towards the door of the flat. "Do we know where we're going?" she asked.

"To the hospital, of course!"

"Yes, but do we know where it is? I mean, there must be several hospitals on this island."

"Then the ambulance station? Let's ask the neighbour!"

The neighbour's broad face lit up with curiosity. "Did you find anything?" she asked.

"No," Josh explained. "We need to phone the ambulance station."

"Come inside," said their neighbour, welcoming them into her own dimly lit and cosy apartment where a thick haze of drying carpet and appetising cooking smells hung in the air. "I'm in a bit of a pickle still, after all that flooding," she explained, finding her way through a swathe of damp clothes piled over tables and chairs. "I've got a phone book somewhere. I just have to find it. Ah! There it is!"

She dialled the number and asked in a loud, firm voice, "Is that the ambulance station?"

They watched as she held the phone to her ear and waited and waited.

When she got through, the conversation went on for some time. She seemed to be explaining the situation clearly enough and was baffled by the lack of response until the point when she asked, "What do you mean? Yes, I'm sure it was blue!"

"She's says that they don't have blue ambulances anymore," she told Josh and Megs, putting the phone down. "They don't know who's taken her."

# CHAPTER EIGHT

"Let's stop here!" said Josh. "I don't feel like going back yet, do you?"

They sat on the grass verge a few yards from the entrance to the hotel.

"I think she's dead," said Megs.

Josh nodded. "It's like what happened in Amaryllis," he said.

"You mean what nearly happened. Of course, we don't know she's dead."

"Good as. What else would they do with her?"

Megs draped an arm around his shoulder. "Poor Josh!" she said, "It never stops, does it? I think we should get out of here as soon as possible." She removed her arm. "Let's face it, you're the main target. You were safer in Amaryllis!"

Josh looked back at the school, just visible through the tall plane trees that lined the empty lane, and then up past the hotel to the garage and shopping centre on the brow of the hill. Feeling a bit stupid in front of Megs, he got up and checked behind the tall beech hedge that screened their view of the hotel.

"He doesn't want us to know something about his past," she said as he returned and sat beside her. "He was adopted, right? I know we've lost the documents, but maybe Sims remembers something about that birth certificate, or maybe we could check the records – wherever they are."

"Do you think we should go back to the apartment?" he asked. "I mean, it's fairly clear she's not coming back. Maybe those photographs would tell us something?"

Megs pointed to her shoulder bag and smiled. "I've got them in here," she said.

"Good thinking," he said. Why hadn't he thought of it himself? His mind spun in all directions. Feathers and his son had known the Prince from the time he started elementary school. Wouldn't that make them a target, too? Yet the Prince seemed more anxious to silence his poor old nanny. What kind of man would do that – send one of his agents to kill the only person who had truly cared for him? Something must have happened during that earlier period that he didn't want known. Maybe those photographs would help them figure out what he was hiding. And what about Sims? He might suddenly remember what was in those documents. What if he was attacked on his way to the hospital?

He felt the reassuring warmth of Megs' arm on his shoulder again. "Come on, Josh!" she said. "What's our next step?"

"Maybe his foster-parents could tell us something."

"Yes, his foster- parents. That's another idea. They still live here. Why don't we visit them? Except -"

"Except what, Megs?"

Megs looked all around her before replying. "We've got to keep this a secret, just between you and me."

"You mean not even tell Feathers?"

"Well, not now, not when Geoffrey's around."

"You don't think Geoffrey...?"

"I don't mean he's a spy," said Megs. She laughed. "I don't think he'd make a very good one, do you? But he doesn't realise how serious this is. You can't blame him! You don't know how many people he's already told. I mean the folder business – everyone knew about that. But what about the nanny?"

Josh thought about it. "Let's speak to Sims again," he said. "Maybe he will remember some of what was in that folder."

"We've got to find him first," Megs reminded him. "What if he's in danger?"

The same thought shot through Josh's mind at the same instant. He pulled Megs to her feet and pointed back the way they'd come. "The hospital can't be far," he said. "It must be somewhere down there past the school."

"Do you think they'd..."

"I don't think so. They stole his folder. That should be enough!"

Josh quickened his stride.

"I was thinking about the nanny," said Megs, hurrying along behind him. "He was very fond of her. Do you think he would really do that – I mean, have her killed like that?"

Josh remembered his brief interview with the Prince. "Yes," he said. "Come on!" He broke into a run.

Just then, he heard a van scrunching on gravel as it stopped a few paces ahead of them. Jason, the young teacher with the floppy black hair, pushed open the passenger seat.

"Come on then if you're coming," he said. "Megs? Is that your name? Hop in the front. Josh, you'll have to shift some of my sports kit and make room for yourself in the back."

"Where are you going?" asked Megs, holding the passenger door open.

"Wherever you want to go! You seem to be going somewhere in a hurry."

"Thanks," Josh called out from the back seat. "The hospital, if you don't mind."

"Oh dear. You're not ill, are you?"

"No, we're meeting Mr Sims there."

The car lurched to a halt. "Oh! Sims is fine. He got back to the school ages ago. He's in the staff room now, chatting with Carol. Have you met Carol? She's fairly new here. Geoffrey will tell you all about her – or maybe not." He laughed.

"His girlfriend?" asked Megs.

"Yes, apparently. She came to return the minibus."

Josh and Megs exchanged glances.

Jason kept the engine running. "Sims didn't tell me he'd been to the hospital," he said. "So, where is it now? The school?"

He made a hasty three- point turn, and the car lurched forward again, travelling a few hundred yards back up the lane and parking beside a large blue minibus outside the school entrance. Megs nudged Josh as soon as they got out of the car. "The ambulance?" she murmured.

"That's the school minibus," Jason explained, following the direction of her eyes. "You know the way from here, don't you? I'll just load my sports stuff into that minibus. I couldn't use it this afternoon. Carol's flat mate borrowed it to move her furniture in."

They found Sims in the staff room, sitting on his own with a cup of coffee in one hand and a pile of exam papers on the table in front of him. He didn't see them at first. They watched as he took a sip of coffee, then picked up a paper from the pile, viewed it at a distance, then grunted and brought it closer to his face. He brought out a red pen, waved it in the air, thought for a bit and assigned the paper a mark. He was on the point of picking up the next script when he looked up and noticed their presence.

"I couldn't find her," he said. "Wrong hospital. I met Carol on my way back and she kindly gave me a lift."

Josh came and sat beside him. "Mr Sims," he began.

"Yes? Did you find Miss Kelshaw?"

"Not yet. Do you remember anything of what was in that folder?"

Sims reached a hand into his jacket pocket, muttered a curse and bent over to retrieve a ball of screwed up paper from the wastepaper basket under the table. "Maybe this list will jog my memory. Hm. School reports. I doubt whether they'd be much use to you. Birth Certificate. Yes. I do remember something there. He was born in Amaryllis. That's handy for you, I suppose. You can obtain the originals. I can't recall what name he went under, but I do know that he had an older brother. That was in the adoption papers. But I don't know anything about him. He never attended our school."

Josh and Megs looked at one another. "Do you know his name?" asked Josh.

Sims shook his head. "I'm sorry," he said. "I don't know that either."

"Mr Sims?" asked Megs.

"Yes, young lady?"

Megs came over and sat on the table, facing him. "We don't know what happened to Miss Kelshaw, but we're very worried. You remember how that folder went missing?"

"Of course, I remember!"

She leant towards him and lowered her voice. "You know that Josh is Pirate Guardian and that the Prince has already tried to kill him?"

"I did hear something about that," he mumbled.

"And there's something funny going on here. You can see that?"

His eyes started to water. "I can see that," he said. "I should never have let that folder out of my sight."

"We're not blaming you, Mr Sims. We trust you."

"Yes, we trust you," said Josh. "But we don't trust anyone else, so we need to keep this a secret."

"And we need to know about Carol's flatmate," added Megs.

Sims stared at the floor. "Poor Miss Kelshaw!" he said. "Do you think she's all right?"

"I'm afraid not," said Megs. "The aim was to silence her."

"We should call the police!"

"Yes, later," said Josh. "Carol's flatmate; do you know anything about her?"

"I never met her. She's only just moved in."

"And she asked to borrow the school minibus?" asked Josh.

"Well, Carol asked on her behalf."

"Do you remember her friend's name?" asked Megs.

Sims rose creakily to his feet and pointed to the staff noticeboard behind him. "It's here somewhere," he murmured. "Ah, here we are. The staff list. Right at the bottom. 'Part-time PE teacher: Kate Kitten.'"

Josh raised his eyebrows at Megs, and she nodded. "We may know her," he said. "Is she tall, with short, fair hair, soft voice?"

"They both are," said Sims. "Carol is new here too, though she's been around for several weeks. She teaches geography – very popular with the boys, I'm told. They're cousins, I believe."

"Two nurses," murmured Megs. "That's what the neighbour said. Maybe we should take a look at that minibus." She turned to Sims. "You see, we think it was used to carry Miss Kelshaw to the hospital," she explained.

"Or dump her," said Josh, standing up.

Sims blinked and stared at Josh in horror. "But she went in an ambulance!" he said.

"That's what we thought too," said Megs, "but ambulances are red, and her neighbour told us she left in a blue van."

"It's true," Sims said with a sigh. "All the ambulances on this island are red."

"And we don't think it was two nurses that entered her house," said Megs, helping the old man to his feet. "Nurses don't normally break locks or empty drawers and make off with the contents."

"Look, I really think we should check that minibus," said Josh, with his hand on the doorknob. He hurried out of the room, leaving Megs and Sims to follow.

His first thought on finding the blue minibus parked in the schoolyard, was relief at seeing it still there. Fortunately, the door of the minibus swung open, and the key was still in the ignition. He climbed into the front seat and checked all the cubby-holes, finding nothing unusual there, though a faint smell of perfume lingered in the air. Was that Carol or Kate? Perhaps they shared the same tastes. Which one was the Cat Lady? Probably Kate, he decided; PE had always been her thing.

He jumped down from the seat and ran round to the back. Megs had already thrown the doors open, and Sims stood behind her, shaking his head and muttering, "You can't trust anyone nowadays."

"No sign of blood," Megs said, peering under the seats, "but there probably wouldn't be, if she was dead by the time that they stuffed her in here."

Sims' blue eyes clouded with doubt as he came to terms with the fact that a murder had just been committed in his own backyard. "Poor Miss Kelshaw!" he said. "And to think that Carol Kitten was in there chatting with me only ten minutes ago. She seemed such a nice young lady!"

The seats in the two front rows were piled high with sports equipment. "Do you think we should remove all this stuff?" asked Megs. "That way we can make a thorough search."

Josh shook his head. "No need," he said. "If you are carrying a body, why not just lay her flat along the space between the seats? Surely that would have been their easiest option... hang on!"

He climbed into the minibus and climbed out again, waving a flowered square of cotton, torn from a dress.

Megs nodded when she saw it and showed it to Sims. "Do you think this belonged to Miss Kelshaw?" she asked him.

"Very probably," he agreed. "That was the sort of thing she liked to wear. I think it's time we called the police."

# CHAPTER NINE

Josh and Megs hung around the staffroom for a while, waiting for the police to return their call about the murder of Miss Kelshaw and the whereabouts of the two 'Kittens'. Poor Sims sat hunched over the table, muttering to himself about how foolish he'd been. "You just can't trust appearances," he explained. "I personally recommended Kate Kitten, despite the fact that she couldn't supply a C.V. She said it got stolen at the airport. And I believed her!"

Megs did her best to soothe him. "She came here to do a job," she said. "She didn't need a C.V. All she had to do was walk into the school and make friends with a member of staff, nick your records from the staffroom, and find Miss Kelshaw's address."

"I suppose you're right," he said, sitting upright for the first time, and looking slightly flushed, like a patient recovering from an anaesthetic. "Well, I won't get taken in like that again!"

"Would you like something to drink?" asked Megs, standing at his shoulder.

Sims thought for a moment. "You'd better not tell anyone else about this," he said, "because one's not really supposed to keep alcoholic drinks in the staffroom, but if you look into that cupboard behind me – not that one – the one on your right, you'll find a bottle of port. I'd like a large glass, if you wouldn't mind. Where's Josh, by the way?"

"He's answering the phone. I think the police must have called back."

Megs sat and watched Sims downing his glass of port. She enjoyed the restorative glow it gave to his features. She looked up to see Josh standing in the doorway. "Any news?" she asked.

"Their plane hasn't left yet," he said. "The police will arrest them at the departure gates and hold them in a cell overnight. They'll call us in tomorrow once they've processed all the evidence against them."

Sims had recovered some of his old bounce by the time they said their goodbyes. They watched him stumble off to his flat on the college grounds and set off down the road.

They found Feathers sitting alone at a round table in the dimly lit reception area of the small hotel, drinking a glass of red wine from a half-empty bottle. He put down the newspaper he'd been reading and rose to his feet, saying, "Ah! The young scamps have returned! I was beginning to think I'd have to eat without you. And that would have been difficult because I've ordered a meal for four. I had to order, you see, because the chef goes off at nine."

"Where's Geoffrey?" asked Josh, as he and Megs sat beside him at the table.

"He had to drive Carol to the airport. Delightful girl, that Carol! Have you met her? I am afraid my son hasn't always been fortunate in his choice of girlfriends. Takes after his father, I suppose. But this one's a stunner. Look! I'll show you her photograph."

Josh and Megs glanced at a picture of a smiling young woman in a bikini who didn't look older than eighteen. Josh tried to imagine what her cousin, Kat – the Cat lady - would have looked like when she was prettier and less catlike. "Why did she leave?" he asked.

"Her mother died unexpectedly," said Feathers. "Most unfortunate. She had to go home for a short while to attend the funeral."

Josh looked at Megs. They both remembered the Cat Lady's story about the funeral of a non-existent aunt. He let the old man ramble on. He didn't look forward to puncturing his illusions.

"Poor Geoffrey was devastated, of course," said Feathers. "Her sister went with her, which must have been some comfort for the poor girl."

"I thought she was a cousin," said Megs.

"No, she was definitely her sister. I never met her, but Geoffrey assured me they were sisters."

*Where was Geoffrey now?* Josh wondered. The plane must have left at least three hours ago. It wouldn't have taken him that long to get to the hotel. Had the Kittens claimed another victim? The Cat Lady must have had time to discover everything he'd learned about the Prince during his schooldays. His life probably hung on how much he knew.

Megs raised an eyebrow at Josh, signalling with her lips that it was up to him to deliver the bad news. But just then a waiter arrived from the kitchen on his left, carrying four steaming dishes on a tray, and Geoffrey emerged from the door on his right – radiant with the good news of his recent engagement to Carol Kitten.

Josh looked at Megs and made a downward gesture with his hands as if to say, *keep a lid on things for the moment*. They sat and ate their meal in silence, leaving father and son to share their joy at Geoffrey's engagement and chat and laugh about a lifetime of shared reminiscences.

At the end of the meal, when Geoffrey got up to leave, Feathers had bad news of his own to tell them. "The Prince has just destroyed the plantations on Windfree," he announced. "You know all those wicked red flowers that have caused us so much harm."

"He said he would do that," said Josh. "That's good, isn't it?"

"Yes, but it will certainly add to his popularity. And that's bad. A number of islanders are already thinking of switching to his cause. Some of the pirates on Colony Island are among them."

Josh had some information he needed to share too, but Feathers hadn't finished. "And Maxtrader's on trial for supplying the dodgy medical trade," he said. "Your friend, John Bosworthy has compiled the evidence."

"But that's good, isn't it?" said Josh.

"In an ideal world it would be," agreed Feathers. "Maxtrader going bankrupt is something we'd all like to dream of. His gunge fields have been destroyed and his only remaining source of income has gone up in flames. He'll probably sit out the rest of his life in prison. In the meantime, what else will fuel our economy?"

"I'm afraid we have a bit of a problem to tell you about, too," said Josh. "Do you remember the Cat Lady?"

Feathers laughed. "How could I forget her?" he asked.

"Do you remember how you found her so charming?"

"Charming? Well, yes, I suppose, at first, I did think that. But she turned out to be a killer!"

"The Cat Lady is Kate Kitten."

"What? Carol's friend?"

"Carol's sister," Josh reminded him. "They were both involved in it."

Feathers shut his eyes for a moment and absorbed the news. "Oh, dear! Oh, dear!" he muttered. "The news will destroy him!"

"The engagement was a sham," Josh said. "They came here on the Prince's orders to dispose of his former nanny and they certainly have no intention of coming back."

Feathers slowly got up from the table. "You young'uns stay here by all means and finish your meal," he said. "But all this bad news is too much for me to handle in one day. I have had a great many near-death experiences in my life, but telling my own son that he's made a mistake of this magnitude is the hardest task I'm ever likely to face."

Megs placed an arm over his shoulder. "Maybe you don't need to tell him," she said. "Let him wait a while for the news to sink in."

He thought about it and shook his head. "No," he decided, "then he'd hear the news from someone else. He'd never forgive me if he realised that I knew and hadn't told him." He stopped on his way up the stairs and said, "I'll tell him first thing in the morning. Best get it over with, I think."

# CHAPTER TEN

Josh tossed and turned in his bed, thinking of that other mind, camped in the wastes of Windfree, weaving his mad schemes to put the Western Isles back to the way they were all that time ago in the days of his famous ancestor, Rupert the Rebel. But the Prince had a guilty secret to hide – one that might ruin his reputation. That's why the Prince had sent his agents to kill Miss Kelshaw. If Josh abandoned his search for the truth, he could become a normal teenager again. If he kept searching, he would be risking his life and other people's lives as well. He'd keep searching, he decided, but he'd do it more carefully next time. With that comforting thought, he rolled over and soon fell asleep.

Megs woke him the next morning with a cup of coffee and a croissant. "They are clearing away the breakfast," she said, "so I thought I'd better bring something up to you before it gets cold." She leant over and gave him a kiss on the lips.

Later, when he thought about it, it was the kiss that did it. She was the only girl that mattered in his life. Why hadn't he thought of that before? All he said at the time was, "Thanks, Megs, that's great. Has Feathers....?"

"Yes, he's gone off to see his son. He says he'll probably be there all day."

"So, we're free! We could -"

Megs smiled. "I don't know exactly what exciting activities you had in mind," she said. She paused. "Is something wrong?" she asked.

"No, please go on," he said, wanting to keep her there a moment longer.

"I was just going to say that the police called. They've arrested the Kittens. They've invited us to call in at the local station. I'd guess what they have to tell us is important."

Josh downed his cup of coffee and leapt out of bed. "Can you call a taxi?" he asked. "I'll be down in a sec!"

As Megs left the room, Josh shoved the half-eaten croissant in his mouth and dashed to the shower-room. Five minutes later, he hurried down the stairs, feeling spruce and clean, and full of curiosity about what he was likely to learn.

Within moments of being dropped off at the police station, Josh and Megs were ushered into a small, comfortable room behind the reception desk, where a large, elderly man in a grey woollen cardigan and steel-rimmed spectacles rose from his armchair and greeted them with a smile.

"Take a seat," he said, introducing himself as senior detective, Michael Denby. "I presume you must be Josh. And I think I know this young lady already. Megs, isn't it?"

Megs blushed at the memory and exclaimed, "You saved his life!"

She turned to Josh and explained, "That time when you were stuck in a room with Fleck, nobody else would listen, but Mr Denby did!" She gave Denby a stare of wonder and awe and said, "You were the only one that listened, and you acted within seconds. I can't thank you enough for that!"

"I suppose I should be the one to thank you," said Josh, feeling a bit awkward and uncomfortable about the incident.

Denby smiled. "Well, I think on that occasion," he said, "we were all saved by the man calling himself the Rebel Prince. He had the man killed – not for your sake, of course- but I don't think anyone was sorry about that."

Josh and Megs exchanged glances. Denby obviously hadn't heard of Fleck's reappearance at the airport. They decided to say nothing.

"Anyway, make yourself comfortable," said Denby, pointing to the three armchairs placed around the table, laden with a selection of soft drinks. "Help yourself to a drink – you can have tea or coffee if you prefer it – and let's move on to the present business." He turned to Josh. "I believe you've already had dealings with Miss Cattermole," he said.

"She tried to kill him twice, Josh," said Megs.

Denby gave her a sympathetic smile. "Well, she would, wouldn't she?" he said. "She's a cat. I believe she nearly killed you too on one occasion?"

Megs nodded and stared at the table. The glint in her eyes suggested that the Cat Lady wouldn't get much sympathy from that direction.

Denby turned to Josh. "I gather the Prince has already made one recent attempt on your life," he said. "Presumably, that's because you are the Pirate Guardian. Can you think of any other reason?"

Megs spoke first. "The Prince knows Josh," she said. "He is very persistent. He will go on investigating the Prince until he finds a flaw in his reputation."

Denby nodded. "That makes sense to me," he said, "which is why he sent the Cat Lady over here to kill Miss Kelshaw." He reached under the table and handed Josh two packages. "There you are!" he said. "I've made copies of the relevant details, so these are for you. We extracted them from Miss Cattermole's baggage; the first contains items stolen from Miss Kelshaw's desk and the second package was taken from the staffroom locker. I think we are doing the Cat Lady a favour in keeping her locked up here; if she returned to Washalot, the Prince would probably kill her for 'letting the bag out of the cat,' in a manner of speaking."

"Is she wearing a circlet?" asked Josh.

Denby shook his head. "The Cat Lady was," he said. "She was immensely proud if it. Mind you, it's no longer just a brass ring fitted round the neck, which you can open with a screwdriver. The variously coloured balls evenly spaced around the rim still dispense pain, release from pain, and death, but I had quite a job dismantling it. I had to do that, you see. Otherwise, the Prince would almost certainly have killed her."

"What about her sister?" asked Josh. "Is she wearing a circlet?"

Denby looked out of the window and paused for thought. Then he came to a decision and said, "That's the thing that first caught my attention," he said. "Carol hadn't even heard about the Rebel Prince and his circlets. She is, in all respects, a perfectly normal young woman. We have been keeping the two ladies in separate cells," he said. "But, reading between the lines, their evidence more or less tallies. I should start by explaining that Carol is a stepsister. The father died some time ago and the cat genes died with him. The mother married a farmer, who lives here in Crown Colony. Carol hasn't seen her sister for several years and she wasn't best pleased to find her landing up at the school where she'd recently obtained a job as a geography teacher."

Josh wondered where all this was leading. "Do you mean she wasn't involved in the murder?" he asked.

"Only in so far as she helped to bury the evidence. Carol claims – and I believe her – that her stepsister simply asked her to bring the minibus. When she saw the body, she didn't know what else she could do."

"She could have-" Megs started to protest.

Denby gave her a thoughtful stare and said, "Yes, she committed a crime, but it wasn't murder. And we have to remember that Kat is her stepsister – and a dangerous stepsister too. The two of them never got on. Besides, Kat had a pistol in her handbag when we arrested her. I have no doubt she would have been prepared to use it on her sister."

Megs shrugged. "Yet Carol was willing to board the plane to Windfree with her," she said.

Denby nodded. "Ah! There you're mistaken," he said. "She chucked her ticket away before we arrested her. She fully expected to be stopped before boarding the plane. That was her escape plan – from her stepsister, I mean."

Josh had sat silent, listening to all this with a sense of relief. If Carol was innocent, or likely to be charged with a minor offence, the wedding might go ahead and Feathers would be a happy man. He wondered whether he should mention the documents stolen from the locker. He noticed Denby's shrewd eyes assessing his doubts.

"Yes, Josh," said Denby. "Carol did steal those documents from the locker. She is afraid of her stepsister, but that's not really an excuse – not in a court of law, anyway. She will have to be punished but I don't want her to lose her job, or her marriage for that matter, so the school has agreed to allow her a four-week leave of absence in view of 'the distressing events she has been through' and I think four weeks in a cell is a satisfactory compromise that the magistrate will be willing to accept. Geoffrey Feathers is with her at the moment, but you are welcome to call in and see her if you feel so inclined."

He looked up, saw the doubt in their eyes, and smiled. "Well, I expect you are eager to get back and find out what was in those documents," he said. "I can give you a summary, if you so wish."

"Yes, please," said Josh, nodding his head vigorously.

"Well, you know that Richard – that was the Prince's original name – never got on with his older brother. Well, his brother – that's Rupert - died in a boating accident. But a couple of bystanders saw the accident and reported that the brother didn't just fall into the water but was pushed. And the Prince – instead of rescuing him – held his head under the water until he drowned. That's fratricide; a crime in any society but the worst crime imaginable in the pirate world."

## Chapter Eleven

They found Feather waiting for them, on the entrance steps of the hotel, shielding his eyes from the afternoon sunshine and smiling at the world like a man who'd just awoken from a bad dream. "So, you've seen Denby," he said, "A great man – don't you think so – full of understanding and common sense? He phoned me to say that Carol was in the clear – well, almost – so that means the wedding can go ahead -"

"In four weeks," Josh reminded him, desperate to get back to Amaryllis.

"Yes, yes, four weeks, but that need not concern us now!" said Feathers, extracting some plane tickets from his top pocket with the triumphant air of a conjurer. "I shall no doubt return for the great event when it's scheduled," he added. "But in the meantime, we have work to do! I have managed to secure a return flight to Amaryllis, via Elephantia, this very evening! I'm already packed, but you two had better get your luggage sorted and clear the room in the next ten minutes. That's when our taxi is due to arrive."

"But what about the main airport?" asked Megs, brushing past him in her haste to get to her room. "Isn't it closed for repairs?"

"Not anymore," said Feathers, rubbing his hands. "Jack Sands has just won the elections. And he'll be waiting there to greet us! Things are happening fast over there in Elephantia, I can tell you!"

They arrived at Elephantia airport, breathless after their sudden departure from Crown Colony, to find the whole place transformed. 'The Unite Party' led by Jack Sands seemed to have changed the atmosphere overnight. The jagged hole in the dome had been covered over with plastic sheeting and all signs of damage in the Arrivals Hall had been swept away. Gone were the long queues in the transit lounge. The officials had been replaced by soldiers; pirates and colonists working side by side, exchanging pleasantries as they checked the passengers through the gates, stood guard at the exits and entrances, or climbed step ladders to paste posters on all the walls.

Josh and Megs stood in wonder, pointing out one caption after another: 'The Unite Party! Let pirates and colonists unite!' read one poster. 'Let the Elephant awake!' read another. 'Better together!' was another popular theme, showing pirates and colonists marching side by side to war. They also saw video displays, one with the caption 'Voyage to the Promised Land' showing colonists wearing helmets and being herded onto ships and another with the caption 'Passport to Slavery' showing pirates being fitted with helmets as they shook hands with the Rebel Prince. One particular video that caught Josh's eye showed a long line of battleships, similar to the one on which he had travelled to Amaryllis, with pirates and colonists waving from the top deck. The caption in this case was 'Windfree – Here we come!'

Megs somewhat spoilt the illusion by peering over Josh's shoulder and asking, "Have you noticed that the sailors in each picture are identical?"

"Well spotted!" said a deep cheerful voice behind them. "You must be Josh and Megs."

They both turned to find a youngish-looking man in jeans and an open-necked shirt, striding towards them, "Feathers has been telling me all about you," he said, giving them each a firm handshake. "I'm Jack Sands. Let's go somewhere quiet where we can talk. Feathers has found a little café over there in the corner. Let's go and join him."

Josh stood in awe of the man's casual confidence and the way he had managed to transform the whole atmosphere of Elephantia overnight. He began to wonder why, at such a busy time, he and Megs had been singled out for such special treatment. The reason became clearer as they followed Jack Sands across the hallway. Some of the onlookers stared and started to whisper. The whisper soon became an excited murmur, and within seconds the murmur became a cheer; "Three cheers for the Pirate Guardian! Hurrah! Hurrah! Hurrah!" Josh turned and waved to the onlookers. Then a voice from the crowd whispered, "And that's Megs! I've read all about her." And another voice whispered, "She was in that competition. Isn't she lovely!" There was another cheer for Megs, and she blushed and waved to the crowd. Josh blushed a little too, feeling privileged to be walking by her side.

Jack Sands laughed and tapped them both on the shoulder. "You see! That's the sound I wanted to hear! There are still plenty of pirates around that believe in their Guardian and the message of peace and harmony. They are not all rushing off to follow the Rebel Prince."

Josh felt inspired by Jack Sand's energy and charisma. But he couldn't help wondering if what he had just seen and heard wasn't a bit too good to be true.

"I know what you're thinking, Josh," said Jack Sands, placing an arm over his shoulder as they approached the café. "What you have seen in this hall is how we would like things to be. As Megs rightly pointed out, we don't have a whole line of battleships. We don't even have one – we had to borrow that one back from Amaryllis. But we have to offer people hope and, to tell the truth, hope is the only thing we've got at the moment. The Prince has been winning this war while we've all been sleeping."

Inside the small café which Feathers had 'found', two soldiers guarded the entrance, armed with rifles, and Feathers sat alone at a round table in the far corner, chatting to another soldier serving drinks behind the bar. Josh and Megs exchanged glances.

"You found them quickly enough!" Feathers said to Jack Sands, as he stood up to greet them.

Jack Sands laughed. "The whole airport found them!" he said, gesturing to them to take a seat at the table. "You must have heard the cheers?"

Feathers nodded. "I don't know how you pulled it off," he said. "The place has changed since our last visit; pirates and colonists working side by side... with so much energy, so much confidence!"

Josh remembered what the lady in the departure lounge had told him. "Is it still dangerous to go into town?" he asked.

"I hear you've sealed off the port," said Feathers.

"That's where most of our troops are engaged at the moment." explained Jack Sands. "Because that's where all the trouble is. Bombs, drone attacks, you name it." He sipped his coffee and added, "Crown Colony has suffered the hardest from bomb attacks. It's now virtually bankrupt."

"What about Maxtrader?" asked Megs.

Jack Sands gave her an astonished stare. "Haven't you heard the news?" he asked. "Maxtrader is dead! He was killed in a drone attack."

Jack Sands looked across at Megs, who'd put her hands to her face to conceal her tears. "I'm sorry. Have I upset you?" he asked.

"We knew him," explained Josh. "Well, it's his granddaughter, Lavinia, we know best."

"I expect you'll be seeing her soon, either here or on Amaryllis. It's no longer safe for Lavinia and her mum to stay in Crown Colony." He turned to Josh and Megs. "Now, Feathers tells me you've both been busy researching the background of the Rebel Prince. There must be something he doesn't want us to know, because he's made several attempts to bury the evidence."

Josh hesitated. "We now know that he killed his older brother in what was supposed to be a boating accident," he said. "That's how he established his claim to be descended from the Rebel Prince."

Jack Sands whistled through his teeth. "Phew! What was his original name?" he asked Josh.

"Richard."

"Right. His real name is Richard, and he killed his own brother. We'll post that information to the media, and it will certainly sway the minds of some of his supporters. Anyway, our real problems lie elsewhere," he added.

"What do you mean?" asked Josh, dreading something bad was about to happen.

"Have you heard of Neustria?"

"The place where the colonists originally came from?"

"Yes, it's a huge continent, far to the south of us. Until recently, we enjoyed friendly relations with their emperor. Not any longer."

"What happened?" asked Megs.

"When the emperor died young, his second wife took over. Some believe she had him killed. The Prince has already been to visit her. We don't exactly know what they agreed, but he has already sent her two boatloads of colonists to work as slaves on her fields. That was the poster you saw, Megs. That one was true! But the emperor has a daughter, a young girl called Prunella..."

"How old?"

"About your age, Megs. By rights, she should be Empress. She was popular in her father's day. She came to our island with the old king two years ago and made quite an impression on the people by her performance in the island games."

"What were her special skills?" asked Josh.

"Archery and long-distance running."

"So, could she help us?" asked Megs.

"We think so. She has escaped, you see, and she must be somewhere in the Western Isles." He looked across the table at Josh. "We are hoping you can help us find her."

## CHAPTER TWELVE

Only a few passengers boarded the flight to Amaryllis, so Feathers headed for an empty row with a window seat, where he could fall asleep, and Josh and Megs piled into an empty row a few spaces behind. Megs sat by the window with a map in her hand, checking all the towns and villages they passed over and finding their names on her map. "Look!" She kept saying. "We'll soon be passing over another town. It's called..."

Josh shut his eyes and pretended to be asleep so that he could think about what Jack Sands had said to him; 'We are hoping you can help us to find her.' But he couldn't do that anymore! He felt like a cheat, thinking of all those soldiers who cheered him at the airport. What were they cheering him for? What kind of Guardian was he? He'd never been that interested in the Piratica and he didn't have anything that made him special anymore; not since he'd placed that necklace in the Temple of Harmony.

Megs nudged him. "Come on Josh," she said. "Are you going to do it?"

"Do what, Megs?"

"Find that girl, of course!"

"Is it so important? What will happen if I find her?"

"Come on, Josh! She's an Empress – or she should be. You don't have to install her on her throne or rescue her from wherever she's hiding, or anything like that. Jack Sands can take care of that. All you have to do is to use your visionary powers to discover where she is."

"But I don't have those powers anymore! I keep telling you that!"

"But you could have if... well, you know."

"If I retrieved the necklace? What are you asking me to do, Megs? My mum would go spare if I did that! She believes in peace and harmony and all that stuff."

"But there isn't any peace and harmony, is there? Things are worse now than they were in the time of Machin."

"Well, I could ask Queen Bellagrossa, I suppose."

"And what if she says 'no'?"

"I don't know, Megs. Let's ask Feathers. He might have some good ideas that we haven't thought of."

Megs patted him on the shoulder and smiled. "I know it's difficult for you, Josh," she said. "Ask Feathers, but I'd think twice before asking the Queen. If she says 'no,' it will make it twice as hard for you to steal it! Think about it!"

Josh did think about it; all day and all night, from the moment they arrived back in Feathers' bungalow in Amaryllis. But the next day, Feathers fell sick and retired to bed, and the doctor arrived, at Megs' insistence, and emptied a spoonful of foul-smelling medicine down his throat and said that the old man was exhausted, and all he really needed was 'a good long rest.'

On the following day, they found Feathers pottering about in the kitchen when they came down to breakfast, humming a sea chanty in his throaty voice as he bent over the frying pan and prepared a substantial breakfast.

Megs nudged Josh and whispered, "Do it now!"

Josh thought he'd wait until Feathers had eaten his meal, but Feathers looked across at them, sensing a conspiracy, and said "If you've got something to say, say it! I'm listening."

"It's just an idea," said Josh. "It can wait until you've eaten."

"What do you mean? I ate breakfast hours ago! This is for you! And by the way, Megs, thank you for all those bowls of soup you brought up to my room; just what I needed! Now, what's on your mind?"

"Thanks, Feathers," said Josh, staring at the plate Feathers placed before him on the table. "I've been thinking about what Jack Sands told me."

"Which bit?" asked Feathers.

"He said 'Find that girl!'"

Feathers nodded. "I thought you'd be thinking about that bit," he said. "But you can't do it, can you? Not without the necklace."

"Do you think it's important, finding that girl?"

"It could be. If she were Empress, instead of that evil stepmother who's obviously in league with the Prince, the balance might swing a bit in our favour."

"I'd have to ask permission from Queen Bellagrossa."

"You could, but she'd certainly say 'no'."

"Is there another way?"

Feathers looked Josh hard in the eye. "There is," he said, "but I suspect you've already thought of it."

"I told him he has to steal it!" said Megs.

"But what if I get caught?"

"Well, you would get caught, wouldn't you? If the necklace goes missing, you would be the obvious suspect. It's no use to anyone else. In that case, I'm afraid, the penalty is death. That's the law over here."

Megs placed an arm on Josh's shoulder. "Then it's no good," she said. "It's too risky!"

"On the other hand, there is another way," said Feathers. "What if nobody knows it's been stolen?"

Josh felt the warmth of that arm defending him from danger. He remembered the stone of knowledge which had been stolen from the museum on Colony Island. "We could replace it with a replica, I suppose," he said. "But that would mean finding a jeweller who could do that sort of thing, and it would have to be a jeweller we could trust."

Feathers laughed and leaned across the table and winked at Megs. "It's obvious that this lad never does any shopping," he said to Megs. "Every shop in town has a replica of the necklace!"

Josh felt a bit of a fool. It was true that he hated shopping – especially going into the kind of shops that sold clothes or souvenirs.

"I've got a replica upstairs in my room," said Megs.

"Well, that solves a problem, providing it's a good replica."

"His mum gave it to me."

"Then it must be good! His mum would never give you anything less than the best."

Megs blushed.

"Of course," said Feathers. "I haven't been to the temple recently, so I have no idea how the necklace is mounted. What about you?"

They both shook their heads.

"Then we'd better check it out. Around lunchtime would be best, because that's when the place gets really busy, so our presence is less likely to be noticed. Better still, I could go there on my own because you two are bound to attract attention. I'll take a photograph- that's what everyone does – and we can study it when we get home."

When they arrived at the top of the steps leading to the temple and found the café where they could sit in the shade of a walnut tree and eat their lunch, two events happened in quick succession that threw all their plans into disarray.

The first was the arrival of Lucy. Josh spotted her, hurrying up the path in their direction with a worn and weary expression on her normally cheerful face. She brightened up a little when she saw them and stood awkwardly at their table, twisting her hands together and saying in a flat voice, "I was told I would find you here."

Megs got up at once and hurried round the table to place an arm round her shoulder.

"Come on, Lucy," she said. "We're all friends here! Tell us what's troubling you."

Lucy started to sob. "It's Gregory," she said in a halting whisper. "My mum and I have got so used to having him live with us. I know he's very old, even for a talking tiger, but he's so funny and kind and loveable. He likes us to sit with him and stroke his fur, and he tells us all those wonderful stories about the old days when the colonists first came to the Western Isles. That's three hundred and seventy years ago, but he remembers it like it was yesterday."

Feathers sighed. "You do when you're old," he said.

"Where is he now?" asked Megs.

Lucy glanced down the path. "He's at home with my mum," she said. "He's not been himself for weeks and I'm very afraid he won't be with us much longer."

Josh jumped up and persuaded her to take his seat. He hurried into the café to buy her a drink. He felt sorry for Lucy, knowing how close she had become to Gregory, having lived with him for over a year now. Thoughts flashed through his mind of his first meeting with Gregory in Amaryllis, and then later in his home on Colony Island. Gregory had become a permanent fixture in his life. He'd scarcely passed a week without seeing him.

Josh waited in line at the bar. He didn't mind waiting there. He understood why Lucie was upset, but he didn't know what to say to her. Megs was better at doing that. Suddenly, out of nowhere, came memories of Gregory talking to the old raven on Discovery Island, chasing that man, Forbes, down the street...

He looked around and noticed a few people whispering to each other and leaving the queue at the bar. By the look on their faces, something serious had just happened. He turned and followed them outside, but couldn't see his friends for a moment because of the crowd surrounding the table. Then, when a few people made way for him, he saw a body lying flat on the ground and Megs kneeling beside it, sobbing.

He stood lost in misery as Feathers put an arm over his limp shoulders and whispered. "It's Lucy. I'm afraid she's been killed. I've no idea why or how. We didn't see or hear anything. Sh! We'll learn more in a moment."

The crowd began to back away as a couple of guards pushed through, carrying a stretcher.

One of them knelt beside the body. After a few checks, he shook his head and said, "There is nothing we can do. She's dead, I'm afraid, but I can't make out what killed her."

Megs leant over the body and silently passed him what looked like a small, winged insect.

"What's this?" he muttered, turning it around in his hands. "It looks like a bee. She wasn't allergic to bees, by any chance?"

"It's one of those artificial bees they use to pollinate the flowers," said his colleague, inspecting the object. "I've read about them. Look! The wings are made of some kind of plastic."

"It's even got a sting," said the first officer, removing an even tinier object from Lucy's arm.

"They don't have stings," said his colleague. "That's what I read about them."

"Well, this one does," said the first officer.

They were both standing up now and showed the tiny 'sting' to Feathers, who grabbed a cloth to hold it with. "Careful!" he said. "This contains a deadly poison. Someone is adapting these artificial bees into weapons of war. What you've got there is a miniature drone; a handheld object which can be directed at a specific person over a distance of... well, I don't know the exact distance, but I suggest the assassin may not be too far away."

Josh walked away in disgust. What mattered was that a kind, loving girl of his own age, full of the vitality you might expect from someone who'd once worn the stone of love, had been picked out, seemingly at random, by a cowardly assassin selecting his target at a safe distance. He felt numb inside. Lucy was so sweet and kind. He wished he had spent more time with her since she'd come to Amaryllis. Why would anyone want to kill her? Then another thought filled his mind with a mixture of fear and shame. If he hadn't given up his seat at that particular moment, the assassin would have killed his intended target, which should have been himself.

# Chapter Thirteen

They found the assassin, a seventeen-year-old lad from Colony Island called Potts, that Josh vaguely remembered from school. Potts handed himself in as soon as he realised that he'd hit the wrong target. He knew what would happen to him once the Prince discovered his mistake.

Two policemen handcuffed Potts and prepared to drive him away to the police station. They asked Josh to come too, as he might have information which would help them check out his story. In fact, Potts proved only too anxious to cooperate once they'd removed his helmet. But since his idea of telling the truth meant telling his captors what they wanted to hear, the questioning went on for three days. Josh returned every evening with new details to report to Feathers and Megs. Potts didn't think the Prince had too many of these 'dart guns.' He had to obtain them from Neustria. He might have as many as ten – well, there could be twenty – they were used to kill important targets like Maxtrader. The police eventually decided that there might be as many as a hundred 'dart guns' widely distributed over the other islands, so they warned every Island Council of the danger of this new form of 'bee sting.'

Meanwhile, Feathers and Megs had been busy with arrangements for Lucy's funeral, and trudged up the hill every day to visit her grieving parents. Lucy's mum could no longer cope with nursing Gregory and running her farm shop alone, and her dad was too old and frail to assist her, so Gregory spent his last days in the bungalow, lying by the fire and snuffling and dozing and telling endless stories about his distant past. Then one morning, quite unexpectedly, he found the strength to rise on his four paws and announce in a trembling, tigerish whine. "I think the time has come for me to say goodbye. I must ask you, my friends, not to follow me on my final journey. I must do what tigers do and go into the woods to die. I have had a long life and an eventful one, and a peaceful death is as much as any tiger could wish."

Released from his prison duties, Josh went up the hill with Megs to talk with Lucy's parents. They all agreed that Lucy would have wished no better end than to be mourned alongside her closest friend. As soon as he heard about this, Feathers advised that, in that case, the funeral would need to be a public event, attracting a large audience. And it would have to be held in the open air, because Gregory's two sons would want to be there, and in the modern world not all the mourners would be comfortable sharing their indoor space with two large tigers. He would have a word with Queen Bellagrossa and see if she would be happy to preside over the event in the Nirvana Stadium.

The mention of Queen Bellagrossa filled Josh with alarm. His stomach churned at the thought of meeting her again, knowing how angry she would be if she knew what he intended to do. And if he tried to avoid her? What then? She'd be crafty enough to suspect there was something amiss. And when Megs mentioned that Feathers intended to inform his parents of the event, he was quick to forestall him. If his parents came over, his mum would get to hear of his plan to steal the necklace, and she'd be angry with him. She'd be angry anyway, once she knew what he'd done, but she'd stick by him. That was her way.

The funeral took place as planned on a Sunday morning in the Nirvana stadium and went on until the early evening, with Queen Bellagrossa seated on her throne, behind a long line of trestle tables, presiding over the event, with Josh and Megs on one side beside Feathers and Lucy's parents on the other. The two tigers sat in front of the tables, licking their paws and gazing at the crowd seated in a semi-circular arena cut into the surrounding hills. As is the pirate way, once Queen Bellagrossa had made her opening speech, members of the congregation would stand up and recall their memories of Lucy or Gregory or break into song to express their grief. Josh stood up and described his first meeting with Lucy and their adventures on Humphries Island, and then he told how Gregory had saved them from the assassins that broke into their house on Colony Island, and how often he had kept them amused on their voyage to Windfree. Megs got up and said that Lucy and Gregory were her two best friends in the world, apart from the boy sitting next to her, and then she had to sit down because she burst into tears. The crowd appreciated that show of emotion and stood up and clapped.

At the breakfast table the next morning, Josh and Megs sat toying with their food in a gloomy and thoughtful mood. They both knew what had to be done and didn't relish the prospect of doing it.

"Are you ready for another trip up the mountain?" asked Feathers.

They both nodded.

"Have you got your necklace and a bag to put it in?" he asked Megs.

"Yes."

"Well, no time like the present. At least it will be cooler at this time of day."

Later, as they started mounting the steps, Feathers announced, "We can't actually do anything straightaway."

"Why not?" asked Josh, desperate to get the whole thing over with.

"We have to check it out, see what tools we may need to extract it without a trace. Besides, there are hardly any people around; that would make us the only suspects."

They stopped for a drink at the table beneath the shade of the walnut tree, then joined a small group of visitors entering the temple. They all seemed to be heading in the same direction; to the room where the necklace stood on display, surrounded by a thin wall of glass.

Returning to their table beneath the walnut tree, they discussed various projects for extracting the necklace and replacing it without being seen. Josh suggested dangling a fishing rod over the screen, but Feathers pointed out that the necklace was clipped to a board cemented to the glass. Megs thought they could somehow pick the lock, but Feathers explained that you couldn't do that because the lock was password protected.

Josh began to suspect that Feathers had a solution up his sleeve, and he wanted to know what it was.

"We must ask Queen Bellagrossa to open it for us," said Feathers.

Josh looked across at Megs and they both gasped their astonishment. Feathers looked unperturbed. "I have an idea that may work," he said. "She comes here every day at about this time to talk with the priests of the temple, so we can but try it."

"But what if she says no?" asked Josh.

"Let's hope she doesn't," said Feathers.

They waited and ordered something to drink and talked about the events at the funeral, until they saw Queen Bellagrossa, heaving her vast bulk up the steps. As soon as she set eyes on them, she headed for their table. She gave Josh and Megs a hug and made a beeline for

Feathers, who stood up to greet her. "Mr Feathers, my old friend," she said "Is pleasure to see you in the face. To me, you look ever younger, no?"

"I'm afraid it doesn't work that way," said Feathers, resuming his seat. "I would like you to see Megs' necklace. Show it to the queen, Megs."

The Queen took one look. Then her mouth opened wide, and a shudder passed through her vast frame. "What you have done?" she demanded. "You have stole the necklace!"

"It's not the real necklace," said Megs. "It's a replica."

Queen Bellagrossa wiped her face with a tissue she extracted from her handbag, and her shuddering ceased. "Is no the real necklace?" she asked.

"But we need the real necklace," said Feathers. "Josh needs it." He explained about the young Empress of Neustria and why discovering her whereabouts was crucial to the defence of the Western Isles, and how only Josh, in possession of the Guardian's necklace, stood a chance of making that discovery.

And slowly the Queen began to listen. "For how long he need it?"

"Maybe a week," said Feathers.

"And I take this necklace?" she said to Megs.

Megs passed over the necklace Josh's mum had given her.

"And you no tell my council?" she asked Feathers.

"Certainly not!" he assured her.

"Wait one moment," she said. "I bring you the necklace."

"She's a reasonable woman," explained Feathers. "She understands why you need that necklace. She just doesn't want her council to know about it."

## CHAPTER FOURTEEN

They walked back to the bungalow in silence. Feathers had a spring in his steps after his triumph with Queen Bellagrossa. Oblivious of the heat, he strode ahead, eager to get home and watch Josh perform miracles. Megs, with the precious necklace in her shoulder bag, struggled to keep up with him. Josh lagged behind, lost in his thoughts.

Home at last, Feathers bustled around the kitchen, enlisting their help as he struggled to prepare a meal. "Josh!" he exclaimed. "Wake up, Josh! We need plates, glasses, knives... You know where to find them! And Megs. I thought we could have a salad. Oh! You're making it! Good!"

Halfway through the meal, Feathers could contain himself no longer. "Josh! You're not wearing your necklace!" he said. "After all this trouble obtaining it, I'd have thought you'd want to try it on and see how it feels!"

Josh cast a sideways glance at Megs, sitting beside him at the kitchen table. She smiled. "I think he needs to be alone for a bit," she said. "As soon as we leave this room, he'll try it. I expect he just doesn't know where to start."

Josh nodded. "If you're looking for a needle in a haystack," he said, "it would help if you knew what the needle looked like and where to find the haystack. I don't know what this girl looks like and I have no idea where to look for her."

Feathers got up from the table. "I think I can help you with that," he said. "I have a picture of Prunella somewhere. It's over a year old, mind you, taken when her father was alive, and she accompanied him on a tour of the imperial provinces. There's a pile of magazines on that corner table by the door. It's in one of them. I'm sure of it."

Megs went to the table and stared at the pile of magazines. "Are they in some kind of order?" she asked.

"What are you asking of me?" asked Feathers. "A miracle of organisation? The dates are on the top right- hand corner of the cover."

It took Megs some time to make a separate pile of magazines that were roughly two years old. "Any other little nuggets of information?" she asked.

"Yes, there's a list of contents on the inside cover. Look for 'Neustria' or 'Prunella' or anything like that."

Megs finally managed to extract twelve magazines from the pile that was two years old. She flicked through the list of contents in each before she exclaimed, "Got it!" She waved the magazine she'd selected and leafed through the pages until she came to the photo they were looking for. "There you are!" she said, placing the open magazine on the table, and pointing to the picture of a girl who looked about twelve or thirteen years old, riding on the back of a camel. "I can't say I like the look of her," said Megs. "She reminds me a bit of the animal she's sitting on."

Josh stared at the photograph. The girl had long, fair hair and a beaked nose, and - unlike the cheerful emperor riding by her side – she wore a bored and disdainful expression, like some rich kid used to being spoilt. But that was before her father died, he thought. If it were true that she'd been kept virtually as a captive by her stepmother for the past year or two, she might have changed; she might even look a bit different. She'd managed to plan an escape. That must have taken some daring. "Do we have any idea where she is now?" he asked Feathers.

Feathers found a map in one of the kitchen cupboards above the sink and laid it on the table. "She has to be somewhere in the Western Isles," he said. "We know she escaped from Neustria, so she must have escaped on the Prince's yacht, since no other ship is recorded in that vicinity at that particular time."

"What did that mean?" Josh wondered. Was she in league with the Prince or was she only pretending? The Prince must have known she was on board; you couldn't hide for long on a yacht.

"So we are looking for a yacht," said Josh.

Feathers laughed. "Hardly!" he said. "If that were the case, the Prince wouldn't be alive today. You can safely assume that as soon as this yacht left the harbour, it travelled in a convoy of much bigger ships, with helicopters circling overhead to protect it from air attacks. The military hardware, of course, was all previously provided by your friend, Maxtrader, in exchange for gunge and medical supplies – in other words, the juice of that little red flower that the Prince has now, thankfully, destroyed."

"Do you know where the ships are heading?" asked Josh.

"We know where they are at the moment," said Feathers. "They are approaching Windfree. But there's something else I've been meaning to tell you. They may not stop at Windfree. There's a strong possibility they are heading for Colony Island. The pirates are winning the battle there and—"

Josh sat up. In a flash of recognition, he remembered his brief meeting with the Prince in his encampment on the isle of Windfree.

At the time, all the vast schemes that the Prince had described in his soft voice had seemed like a madman's fantasies. But, one by one, they had all happened! And now he intended to land on Colony Island – just as he'd promised – and rebuild the castle of the original Rebel Prince.

"But my parents -?" he cried in alarm.

"Yes, Josh, that's another thing I've been meaning to tell you," said Feathers. "The news only came in yesterday. Your parents are already in Elephantia. And they will shortly be with us in Amaryllis."

Well. That was good, but in a way, not so good. Josh wasn't sure how he felt about his parents arriving at this particular moment. He knew he'd have to explain to his mum about the necklace, but not now when he needed to learn all over again how to use it.

"What about Sandy?" asked Megs.

Feathers nodded. "Yes, Sandy and his parents are in Elephantia, along with many more of your friends from Colony Island. They may opt to stay there to assist in the resistance movement. If a full scale war breaks out in the Western Isles. Elephantia may prove the safest place to be."

"Why not here?" asked Megs.

"Here? In Amaryllis?" Feathers shrugged. "Rumour has it that Neustria has formed an alliance with the Prince," he said. "If that's true, their troops could swarm over all these little isles that lie within reach of its northern shores."

Josh got the message. "I think I'll go upstairs and try out the necklace," he said.

Megs removed it from her bag and placed it around his neck. "Don't worry if it doesn't work first time," she whispered in his ear. "You haven't worn it for a year. It will take getting used to again."

Josh realised, as he climbed the stairs, that he had never really got used to wearing the full necklace with its three onyx stones. He had only used it twice, as far as he could remember. He wondered if it had even greater potential than the single stone of truth, which had helped him countless times to survive the battle against Machin.

He sat on the bed with a picture of that girl in his head. He tried to imagine what she would look like when she was two years older; still slim and with long fair hair but taller and probably wiser – not proud and pampered, as she might have been when she was being brought up as the future Empress... but a prisoner on a ship far from home. He felt the stones in the necklace buzz a little and then go dead.

Then he thought of the Prince. The effect was immediate and almost overpowering in its intensity.

*With a clarity that he'd never quite experienced with the single stone, he found himself standing in the dimly lit cabin of a yacht. He had to bend his knees to maintain his balance as the floor swayed with the undulating motion of the waves. And the four figures in the small cabin were too close for comfort. It was hard to believe they'd be unaware of his presence if he stumbled into them. He instantly recognised the two figures seated on a bench on the other side of the cabin, the ugly giant and the small man at his side. They were Osborne and Miggs. He was glad they were wearing circlets. If anyone deserved to wear circlets, those two did! His gaze shifted to the two figures seated at the table playing chess, the tall figure of the Prince, wearing his white robe with the purple lining, and the slim figure of the girl with fair hair, wearing a pink tee-shirt and jeans.*

*It was the girl's turn to move. Josh had been the school champion at chess, but this girl was out of his league. In three quick moves, which the Prince cautiously responded to, she had arranged her pieces on the board, so that the next move from her knight would place his king in check. And the next move from her queen would place his king in checkmate. But she didn't make those moves. Instead, she placed her queen in a vulnerable position. The Prince took the queen with his* bishop, and in a few swift moves, the girl ended up losing the game. "Silly me!" she sighed, pushing the board aside. "You always win!"

"You always let me win!" murmured the Prince.

"Had he rumbled her?" Josh wondered. He dismissed the memory of that girl on the camel. This girl was modest and intelligent, and a sharp judge of character, too. She'd played on the Prince's vanity. That man could never really believe that anyone was cleverer than himself. So she'd judged the situation just right. She'd shown she could be a useful ally; not stupid, but modest enough to do what was asked of her. What was her game? Was she hoping that the Prince would help her regain her throne? Or was she just secretly plotting her escape?

"What game are we playing now?" she asked the Prince, fixing her steady gaze upon him like the child she pretended to be.

He handed her a sheet of paper and a pen. "This one's called 'Guess Who?'" he said. "I want you to draw me a picture, and I'll try to guess who it is."

She sucked the end of her pen, bent in concentration over the page and handed him a neat picture of a small woman with big eyes and a pointed hat, wearing handcuffs attached to a chain and being led away by a little girl with the words 'tra-la-la' in a bubble rising from her mouth.

"I don't think I get any prizes for guessing that one," he said. "That's your stepmother. Would you like me to help you make that happen?"

She nodded like a little girl half her age and asked, "What are we doing tomorrow?"

"Tomorrow morning," said the Prince, "we will arrive in Colony Island where my friends over there spent their childhood. Isn't that right, Miggs?"

"Yes, sir."

"And Osborne?"

*"Yes, sir."*

*"Right, you two, go out and attend to the sails!"*

*He turned to Prunella. "I'm off to bed, and I think it's time for you to do the same. I wish you good night."*

*"Good night" she said, and as the Prince turned to leave the cabin, Josh thought he heard her murmur something under her breath that sounded like 'and good riddance.'*

He placed the necklace in the top drawer of the desk beside his bed and went downstairs. He found Megs and Feathers in the sitting room, open-mouthed and eager to pounce on him with excited questions.

"That didn't take you long!" said Feathers. "What did you see?"

Josh described the scene in the cabin. "She's not at all like you imagined!" he said, turning to Megs. "She's modest but intelligent – incredibly intelligent! I think she's got the measure of the Prince." He described her moves in the game of chess.

"Is she in danger?" asked Feathers.

Josh hesitated. "I'm sure she would be if he saw her game," he said.

"How do you know it's a game?" asked Feathers.

Josh mentioned the picture she'd drawn and the words he thought she'd uttered after the Prince left the room. "I think she wants him to oust her stepmother and replace her on the Neustrian throne."

"Would he do that?" asked Megs.

"He would if he thought he could control her," said Feathers. "The stepmother drives a hard bargain. I'm sure he'd much rather have someone young and innocent running the place on his behalf."

"She's certainly not innocent!" said Josh. "But he thinks she is, and he seems to like her."

Megs mentioned all those colonists wearing circlets and labouring on the Neustrian estates. "Do you think she'd change all that?" she asked.

Josh had to admit that he didn't know. He didn't think that she liked the Prince, but that didn't mean that she was on any other side except her own.

# CHAPTER FIFTEEN

The next morning, having tossed and turned all night, with the image of the Prince and that girl at the chess table running through his dreams, Josh felt anxious and impatient. The power of that necklace sent a nervous shimmer through his veins. He felt he could do some good with it, if only he knew where to focus his attention. He realised he needed advice.

He found Feathers sitting in the garden with Megs. Feathers liked to start his mornings by listening to the news on the radio, and then checking the reports in the local newspaper.

"How are things today?" asked Josh.

"Things?" asked Feathers, tossing his paper aside and glaring at Josh as if he were mad to ask such a question. "I'd say things were pretty desperate. Colony Island has just surrendered to the Prince."

"But what about all those colonists on Colony Island – and some of the pirates there too?" asked Josh. "Didn't they put up a fight?"

"Most of them did," said Feathers, "and now they're all wearing circlets."

"And where are they now?"

"They are being loaded onto barges as we speak and sent off to work in the fields in of Neustria. That's the deal the Prince made with the Empress."

"I've been thinking," said Megs, turning to Josh. "You know those circlets? Do you remember how Sandy once showed you how to open them?"

Josh shook his head. "That won't work any longer," he said. "They're secured by a lock."

Megs thought again. "Well, what about the last time you wore the Guardian's necklace, and the Prince was wearing a fake one and you were able to break it, just by using the power of the stones? Could you do that?"

"Let me think, Megs."

He thought of those barges bearing captive colonists away to Neustria. There must be a captain on board controlling the circlets. What if he could locate his device and disarm it? That would give a shipload of – say - two hundred fighting men the chance to seize control of their ship and rejoin the fighting forces.

He looked up to see Feathers and Megs watching him intently. "It sounds like an idea," he said. "I could at least try with one of the first barges moving out of the harbour."

"Hold on! Let's think this thing through," said Feathers, sitting bolt upright. "What if the Prince, or one of his inner circle, watching events from afar, realised what was going on and warned every other barge in the vicinity?"

"Why? What could the commanders do?" asked Megs.

"They could press the 'destroy' button and kill all the men under their command."

"Would they do that?" asked Josh. He knew instantly what the answer would be.

"Yes," said Feathers, "if the Prince ordered them to do it."

There was a long silence. Then Feathers said, "On the other hand, there can't be more than about ten barges heading from Colony Island to Windfree." He rubbed his hands at the prospect of action. "I can get their exact location and provide you with their positions on a map. I can also inform the Council of our plan and ask them to send a battleship to pick up the crews and remove their circuitry – thus providing our friends in Crown Colony with two thousand able-bodied fighting men. It's an awful risk, so let's wait for the council to decide. And by the way, Josh," he added, as he got up to go to the phone. "I wouldn't start from Colony Island. I would start from the opposite direction. That way, our plan is less likely to attract immediate attention."

Josh and Megs sat around in the garden, not speaking much, and jumping up every time they heard Feathers get off the phone. Then another phone rang, and he answered it, and that phone was swiftly followed by another. Josh thought he'd counted ten phone calls before Feathers appeared through the French windows, mopping his brow, and saying, "Finally, they've agreed!"

Feathers unrolled a map of the islands and pointed out the current positions of each barge – "That's where they are now," he added. "They will have moved south a bit by the time you find them."

Josh took the map and prepared to go inside. Megs whispered "good luck" in his ear and gave him a hug. It was the hug that did it. He ran up the stairs.

His first thought, as he sat on his bed and extracted the necklace from the top drawer of his desk, was to focus on a place he knew well; the main harbour of Windfree where he'd landed on his visit to the Prince. He was there in a flash, observing an empty stretch of ocean. But as soon as he checked the map, the stones in the necklace followed his thoughts. He was up and away again, zooming in on a flat-bottomed barge crammed with rowers armed with circlets, forging its way through the waves. A pirate stood at the helm, shouting commands. And in his hands lay a small flat plastic device. Josh focussed his mind on that device and heard a tiny 'phut' as the plastic melted and fell from the man's hand. But the crew were too busy rowing to notice what had happened and simply went on rowing. He assumed they'd discover their release in time. He had to move on.

He soon found that the map had ceased to matter. The necklace had seized what was in his mind, and that was enough. The next target had come into view, and he quickly disarmed it. But the next target didn't have a commander. He'd already been disarmed! The necklace had apparently grasped the general principle by this stage and needed no further prompting. It wasn't long before Megs rushed into the room. "Stop! You don't have to do any more, Josh!" she cried. "They've all been disarmed!"

Josh slipped the necklace back into the drawer and followed Megs back into the garden where Feathers, with a huge smile on his face, patted Josh on the back and said, "Your idea worked! The Council is delighted! They are already picking up the crews and transferring them to Crown Colony, where they'll have their helmets removed and be fed and rested until they're fit enough to join the armed forces."

Feathers paused and added in a serious voice, "That's the good news, at any rate."

"What's the bad news?" asked Josh.

"We have to move to Crown Colony."

"Why?"

"Everyone, including the Prince, now knows that you have the necklace. That hasn't gone down well with Queen Bellagrossa, who is answerable to her council."

"But why Crown Colony? Why not Elephantia?"

"Because that's where you are needed, Josh. You've given the game away. Everyone now knows what the necklace can do!"

# Chapter Sixteen

A soldier armed with a rifle saluted them as they stepped off the plane in Elephantia. He led them to a parking lot at the edge of the runway, where two familiar figures stood beside a camouflaged army lorry waiting to greet them. Josh looked around for a sign of his parents, disturbed not to find them waiting there.

General Fairbones approached with the aid of a walking stick and shook Josh's hand. He looked even more like an elderly badger. "A wonderful achievement, freeing those men on the barges," he said. "It's greatly improved morale over there in Crown Colony. That's where we're going now, of course. Your parents wanted to come and greet you, but I told them we won't stay there long. It's too dangerous!"

"Is his mum still mad with him?" asked Megs.

"Why, of course, this is Megs!" he exclaimed, shaking her hand too. "I didn't recognise you at first – though I should have done, because I remember you well enough. Now, in answer to your question, of course, his mum's not angry with him! He had to do it, you see – steal the necklace- well, I don't really call it stealing - and look how useful it proved!"

"Will we see Sandy?" asked Megs.

General Fairbones laughed. "Sandy and his dad are coming with us!" he said. "If you look at that lorry, you should just be able to spot them. They've chosen to sit at the back as they need a lot of leg room."

Feathers stepped forward to shake hands with the general. "You don't know me," he said in his deep voice. "I'm Feathers."

"Yes, but I know <u>of</u> you," said Fairbones, squeezing his hand. "You're the famous explorer. And I expect you have a different challenge on your hands now, taking care of these young tearaways!" He looked serious for a moment and said, "We have to go to Crown Colony to give the troops moral support, but I have to warn everybody – especially Josh – that we will be flying into danger. The Prince knows that Josh has the necklace now, so he will do everything in his power to hunt him down and kill him. Sorry! That's a fact which needs to be said. So, it's up to all of us – and that includes the soldiers sitting in that van – to ensure that doesn't happen."

Jack Sands, who'd been standing in the background, stepped forward at this point, smiled, looked at his watch and said "I agree with everything that the general said. Now, let's get started."

Jack Sands indicated that Josh should go first, so he mounted the step behind the driver's seat, with Megs close on his heels, and they hurried past several rows of soldiers and found a space on the back seat beside Sandy and his dad. Feathers got in last and sat in front behind the driver. Josh could just see the top of his head bobbing up and down as he chatted with the general and Jack Sands.

Josh reckoned that Sandy had grown six inches since he'd last seen him, and he looked more solid and confident. "I suppose, if the Prince wanted to kill you, he'd do it now," he said in his flat voice.

"You normally start a conversation by saying 'hello,'" said his dad, in the window seat beside him.

"Oh, hello," said Sandy. "Sorry. I forgot that bit."

"Hello!" said Josh. "Why would the Prince attack now?"

Sandy turned and gave him a thoughtful stare with his clear blue eyes. "Well, he could not only kill you but the two leaders of the resistance," he said. "He probably knows where we are and, for all we know, one of those planes circling overhead could be his…"

"Stop trying to frighten us," said Megs. "Anyway, you haven't said hello to me, yet."

"Oh yes. Hello," said Sandy, blushing. "Of course, for all we know, one of these soldiers may be secretly working for the Prince. He could have one of those circlets – not wearing it, because that would be obvious, but stuffed up his shirt."

"Well, he seems to have missed his chance!" said Megs, standing up. "We're about to get off! Look! There, on the runway! That must be the plane that will take us to Crown Colony."

On board the plane, Josh found himself sandwiched between Sandy and his dad. "We'll be staying at the Fairways Hotel," his dad informed him. "I believe you're familiar with the place. Some of the troops are billeted at Portlands College nearby. These are the men you rescued from the barges, so they're raring for a fight with the enemy. I wouldn't take too much notice of Sandy's warnings."

At that moment, Jack Sands pressed a button on his phone and the words of a popular song rang out through the van.

*"Has everyone heard of the Rebel Prince?*
*He killed his own brother. Yes, that's what he did!*
*He drowned him at sea. The poor little lad.*
*And you know what came next, if you think that was bad?*


*His real name's not Rupert! He used to be Dick!*
*Yes, he used to be Richard. That's what he was called!*

*He killed his own brother. Now, ain't that a shame?*
*He's only a Prince by stealing a name!"*

The song went on through several verses, to the raucous joy of the soldiers in the van.

"So your researches weren't entirely wasted," Sandy's dad said to Josh. "The singer's Andy Jones, by the way. He is very popular at the moment. That song's done wonders for morale, and they say it's won over more than a few pirates to our cause."

Josh gave a grin of satisfaction. "Are we landing in Paradise City?" he asked.

Sandy's dad laughed. "That place is hardly paradise now," he said, "not that it ever was! The rebel troops have completely taken over there - pirates from Windfree and Humphries Island, as well as a few of our own. The whole of the west of the island is now a no-go area. We're digging in over there in the east and have gained a little ground recently, but not much."

The small plane bumped down on the playing fields of Portland College and Josh and Megs found themselves sandwiched between two tall soldiers and hurried along the familiar path to the Fairways Hotel.

The manager of the hotel gave them a nervous welcome. "He's pleased to have so many guests," Feathers whispered in Josh's ear. "But he's worried that this may make us subject to a bomb attack."

Jack Sands stood at reception, chatting with the manager, and assigning people to their rooms. Josh hurried up to his room, sat on the bed, and retrieved the necklace from his rucksack. He had to know if the Prince had arrived in Crown Colony and, if so, what he was planning. The question burned so intensely in his mind that the necklace responded instantly.

*He found himself transported to a strangely familiar scene. He could tell from the rolling motion of the floor beneath his feet that he'd landed in the cabin of a boat, but one much larger and more lavishly furnished than the previous one. The Prince had installed himself in Maxtrader's yacht!*

*Zooming in closer, he could see that the Prince had abandoned the simple life he led on the island of Windfree. He had grown fatter and more arrogant – you could see it in his eyes. He had chosen to sit where Maxtrader sat before him, in a comfortable high- backed armchair at the head of the long table, where he could beckon to his advisers or dismiss them with a nod. And these must be his trusted lieutenants; none of them wore helmets with circlets!*

*The Prince sat there like a contented spider in the largest boat in Crown Colony's principal harbour, transformed by all the power at his disposal. He had a large map spread out on the table in front of him, and each time an adviser stepped up to the table, he would stare at the map, point to a specific area, and mark it with a cross. Josh imagined that the fate of thousands depended on that little cross.*

*What were they discussing? Josh knew he had to get closer, but what would happen if he bumped into someone in this crowded cabin? He took a cautious step forward, but at that precise moment, a tall pirate changed direction and walked straight through him. He'd known all along that he was an invisible presence, but it was an odd way of having it confirmed. He walked forward with confidence, as if the people in that cabin were shadows, and he alone was real.*

*He found a seat almost within touching distance of the Prince and listened as a pirate he thought he recognised – an elderly lieutenant he'd seen issuing orders at the Prince's camp in Windfree – came and whispered in the Prince's ear "What have you done with the girl?"*

*The Prince laughed. "The young Princess Prunella, you mean?" he asked. "She's retired to her cabin. Political discussions can be tiring for young ears. Besides, there are some things said in this room that we might not want her to hear."*

*"But can we trust her? Wouldn't it be wise to fit her up with a circlet?"*

*"Oh, I think we can trust her. She's very level-headed, and she understands the idea of mutual advantage. I'm planning to restore her to her empire; isn't that what they call a win-win situation? Fitting her up with a circuit might give people the wrong idea. After she's installed on the imperial throne, I'm sure she'll do what she's told."*

*Josh felt a thrill of excitement. What if the Prince had made a mistake? What if that girl hadn't gone to her room but chosen this moment to escape? He thought of her performance at the chess table. Where was she now?*

*The necklace needed little prompting. The new scene that opened up before his eyes was a cliff path. He reckoned he had to be standing somewhere along the north coat. He only managed to catch a glimpse of her because she was half-hidden by the yellow gorse bushes that grew on either side of the path. Looking back from the point where she was standing, he could just make out the harbour where the yacht was moored. So, she hadn't gone far, but it was clear where she was heading. If she managed to walk a few more miles without getting caught, she'd reach the lands controlled by the resistance fighters. She'd never manage that without their help!*

Josh took off the necklace and sat for a moment on his bed. He knew this time that he faced a challenge which he couldn't achieve on his own. He needed the consent of Feathers and the leaders of the resistance army, and he needed to tell Megs – that went without saying. But all this had to be done quickly, because in a few minutes, the Prince would learn that the girl was missing and then the hunt would begin.

He knocked on Feathers' door and, before Feathers could say anything, he whispered, "The girl's escaped. I can't say anything because I don't have time to repeat things to the general or Jack Sands. Can we meet downstairs in a few minutes?"

Feathers nodded. "I'll pass on the message," he said.

Josh knocked on Megs's door and explained what he'd just seen. They found Feathers talking with the general and Jack Sands downstairs in the restaurant. The three men stood over a map spread out on a table in the far corner.

"Put on your necklace!" said Jack Sands.

Josh did as he was told.

"Where is she now?"

Jack Sands handed him a pencil, and he marked a spot on the cliff path.

"And where is the Prince?"

"Hang on a moment... he's talking to his advisers. I think he's just discovered that the girl's gone missing. They're talking about sending out planes, troops, a search party on foot..."

"Ok. Stop that now. Concentrate on the girl! And keep us posted."

Jack Sands turned to the general. "Any ideas?"

"A diversion," said the general. "Our closest troops are those men from the barges."

"If we transport them to here," he drew a cross on the map a few miles inland, "they can attack the enemy at their weakest point, and possibly break through their lines."

"And what about air cover, for the search, I mean?"

"No use," said the general. "They would simply attract attention. We want the enemy to focus on our frontal attack. We just need our small elite force, the ones upstairs, to head for the cliff path and attempt to rescue the girl."

"Good," said Jack Sands. "Let's put that plan into action."

"I'll go over to Portlands and prepare the troops," said the general. "And Feathers, I'd be grateful for your help."

Feathers nodded, and the two men left the room.

Jack Sands turned to Megs. "Can you run upstairs? Just knock on every door and tell our men to meet here in the restaurant. You don't have to enter the rooms. Just shout. And as soon as the first men emerge, I expect they'll help you."

Megs was already halfway out of the restaurant by the time he turned to Josh. "I need you here and I need you there," he said. "You are our eyes and ears, so you are the only one who knows what the enemy are doing and where to look for that girl. So, I need you here. But, I suspect the girl knows who you are, and she is more likely to feel safe with you and Megs than if she finds herself surrounded by strange soldiers, who could be the enemy as far as she's concerned. Are you with me?"

"So we'll go with the soldiers?" asked Josh, with sudden pride at being included in the adventure.

"Yes, but I need you to wear that necklace and report back every time you learn more about the whereabouts of that girl or her pursuers."

## CHAPTER SEVENTEEN

J osh sat beside the driver, put on the necklace, and searched for that
girl. What was she doing now? She had reached a headland, where
the path bent inwards – perhaps five miles from their hotel. But she
was panting now, and her pale face trembled with uncertainty. Her
eyes darted to her left, and she took a sudden dive through a gap in
the gorse bushes and lay there trembling. He turned to the driver of
the lorry and pointed to her position on the map.

The driver nodded and said, "That's inside enemy territory. We'll
have to stop in a bit and hunt in pairs. Any news from our little army
of ex-bargemen?"

"I'll have a look. They're cheering about something. I think they've
broken through."

"Good. That will keep the enemy troops busy."

Josh noticed something else that filled him with hope. Most of the
retreating enemy soldiers wore helmets with circlets. He saw one of
them train his rifle on his controller. Another had already done the
same. It might not have been as neat and precise a way of disabling
the controls, but it had the same effect. And the idea seemed to have
caught on. All along the enemy lines, he could see soldiers in helmets

throwing down their rifles and holding their hands up high in a gesture of surrender.

*Why hadn't anyone thought of this before?* he wondered. If you had a pistol, or even a knife, you didn't need to disarm the little gadget in the man's hands; you just had to kill the man that controlled it. The danger, of course, was that another commander would see what you were up to and press the destroy button. Then you'd have two hundred deaths on your conscience.

Josh phoned through the news to Jack Sands and switched his attention back to the girl. She hadn't moved from her position in the undergrowth, but he spotted soldiers forming a wide circle round her hiding place and slowly moving in. And these men were sworn enemies! They weren't wearing circlets. Two soldiers stood barely a mile from their position, so he advised the driver to stop.

He quickly drew a circle on the map, marking the rough position of the enemy soldiers.

Then, when everyone emerged from the van, he showed them the map and pointed out where the girl was hiding. The oldest member of the group, who seemed to be in charge, told his comrades to hurry forward, making no noise, and stopping every time he raised his hand, so that Josh could advise them of any change in the enemy position. They had to move fast, because the enemy were closing in on their target, and they had to move silently. If they encountered the enemy, and if they had no choice but to kill them, they had to do that in silence too, because the slightest sound would attract more enemy soldiers to join the search.

Josh and Megs jogged along as best as they good behind the elite team of soldiers, who raced effortlessly ahead through the trees and undergrowth. "It's no use, Megs," said Josh, panting to a halt. "I have to check this thing, anyway, to see if anything's changed up ahead.

Our soldiers will slow up soon, as they near the target area. We'll catch up with them in the end."

Megs smiled and sat on a fallen log. "It's gone well so far," she said.

*Don't say that, Megs*, he thought, as he made another search for that girl. What if she made a dash for it? Then, they would surely catch her! But she hadn't moved. She'd simply buried herself deeper in the undergrowth. And he saw that she had a bow over her shoulder and a sheath of arrows strapped to her side. She didn't mean to give herself up without a fight.

He looked around for her searchers. They had taken their time. He reckoned there were twelve of them, which meant that each one had a large area to search. It would get easier as they tightened the circle.

He reported back to Jack Sands, then grabbed Megs' hand and pulled her up from her log.

They raced along together to catch up with the soldiers waiting up ahead. Conversation was in whispers now as they were nearing their target. Josh showed them the map with the new dispositions of the enemy soldiers, and their leader whispered, "Right, my target is five hundred yards at 12 o'clock. The rest of you fan out in a circle and close in on your targets. Not too closely, mind! It's better to let them wait for you than risk raising the alarm."

He turned to Josh and Megs. "You two follow me at a distance. I'll give you a wave when my target's been sorted."

"12 o'clock means straight ahead," said Josh. "We might as well wait here for a bit where we can't be seen. Then we won't have to crawl like him through the undergrowth." He took another look at what was happening ahead of him. The girl hadn't moved. He admired her coolness. Many people would have made a sudden rush for freedom. But those people would be dead.

The circle around her hiding place had tightened. The soldiers from the van were hard to spot because they were crawling through the undergrowth, but he spotted a few of them all closing the distance on their quarry. Finally, he stared straight ahead of him, and saw the leader waving him forward.

"It's a messy business, killing people," said the leader, when they caught up with him. "But if they won't give in when you ask them nicely, what else can you do?" He pointed to the body lying prone in the grass and said, "Let's move on. There's no crawling required now. Judging from the silence, the rest of the targets are probably dead. I'll just make a call to the driver and tell him to come closer, in case we have to make a quick getaway."

Together, they walked silently, first through the bracken and gorse, then through the woods until, on all sides, they could see other members of their team closing the circle around the hiding place. When they finally reached within calling distance, the leader asked Josh to walk ahead with Megs. "I don't want to frighten her," he explained. "If she sees a lot of soldiers, she might scream or try to escape. It's best if you two speak to her first."

Josh stepped forward and called out. "Hi, Prunella, you're safe now. I'm Josh and this is Megs, and we have come with a small group of soldiers to rescue you."

A slim figure in a pink tee-shirt with fair hair entangled in brambles emerged from her hiding place. "Are you the boy with the necklace?" she asked in a level voice.

"Yes," he said.

"You'd say that even if you weren't," she said. "But I'm inclined to believe you. And who's this?"

"Don't you mean 'who are you?'" asked Megs.

Prunella blushed. "I'm sorry," she said. "I didn't mean to be rude. I have to improve my manners. I know that." She stepped forward and shook Megs' hand and Megs was so pleasantly surprised that she gave her a hug.

"We've learned a valuable lesson," said Jack Sands, as soon as they all arrived back in the hotel lounge, congratulating the young Empress, Prunella, on her daring escape, and chatting about the success of their rescue campaign. "And we've learned something else, too. The Prince can be defeated. We have already seen how two thousand men, released from bondage, have surged forward and recovered vast swathes of enemy territory, aided by almost as many men who have taken their freedom into their own hands by shooting their controllers."

Everyone broke into cheers. But Jack Sands held up a hand in a plea for silence. "However, there have been casualties, I'm afraid," he said. "Two hundred brave men, who saw their comrades achieve freedom by shooting their controller, got there seconds too late. The controller pressed the destroy button and those men are now dead."

The room went silent as Jack Sands added, "I think we can say no more on this subject except that it would be foolish for us to urge those men to seek their freedom in this way because the dangers are obvious. I think we must leave it to their individual consciences. Finally, I must tell you that the lorry is waiting to take us to the airport in ten minutes' time, so if you haven't already packed, I would urge you to do so."

Josh overheard Prunella whispering to Megs. "Do you think I could get something to eat?"

Megs grabbed her hand. "I've got a bit of food stashed away in my room," she said as she led her up the stairs. "You never know what will happen next with this lot. And you can have a shower and change into some of my clothes if you want. We're almost the same size."

# Chapter Eighteen

As soon as Josh landed in Elephantia, his mum ran forward and threw her arms round him.

He breathed a huge sigh of relief when she whispered in his ear, "You did the right thing with that necklace!" Then she said out loud so that everyone could hear, "You'll have to be doubly careful now, because the Prince will stop at nothing to have you killed." She turned to Jack Sands, standing behind her. He nodded in agreement and wished them all a good flight to Amaryllis.

"But what about Queen Bellagrossa? Won't she call me before the council?" he asked.

"That's all been sorted," said his dad, with his usual cheerful optimism. "The Queen, as you know, is a great believer in what she calls 'demogracy'. The counsellors that disagreed with her are in prison, but she has promised to let them out, and even give them something to eat, once they admit their mistake."

His mum had already turned her attention to Prunella. She put her arms around her, and praised her for her bravery, and promised that as soon as they arrived in Amaryllis, she'd love to know more about her adventures.

Josh was afraid the girl would burst into tears. He didn't know quite what to make of her. He'd seen how she could reason things out like an adult, but in other ways, she seemed a bit reserved and awkward with people she didn't know. "Leave her to Megs, mum," he suggested. "They're dead set on sharing a room together. I'm sure she'll have lots to say in due course."

Megs grinned, and his mum quickly backed off. "That's great," she agreed. "I couldn't ask anything better for her."

Josh sat beside his dad and dozed off on the flight to Amaryllis. He awoke to hear his dad saying that there wouldn't be room in the bungalow, so they'd found "a nice little cottage for themselves, with a garden, just a bit further up the road." He breathed an inward sigh of contentment. Much as he loved his parents, he'd grown used to the freedom that living with Feathers entailed.

They took a taxi up the hill to the bungalow. Megs got quite excited as she pointed out all the sailing ships in the harbour and the orange trees that lined their route up the hill. Prunella looked pleased, too. She said it reminded her of her last journey with her father before he was killed.

"I thought he was stung by a bee," said Megs.

"So did I at the time," said Prunella. "I now know it was a miniaturised drone. That's what I learned from the Prince."

Josh's parents went silent, absorbing the news.

Then Megs broke the silence as the taxi approached the bungalow. "There you are!" she said, nudging Prunella. "That's where we live!"

"I think I know what the Prince will do now," said Prunella in her level voice, "He will have someone waiting inside the house to kill you."

Josh instantly saw her point.

"Put on your necklace!" urged Megs.

He didn't need any prompting.

The taxi stopped outside the bungalow, and nobody got out. With the aid of his necklace, Josh saw a man in blue overalls moving around the kitchen. He couldn't make out what he was doing in there, but it involved uncoiling a long length of wire and what looked like a timepiece which he seemed to be busy adjusting.

"There is a man in there," warned Josh. "He seems to be packing up now. Can we stop him before he comes out?"

"I'll just have a quiet word with him," said Feathers, easing his heavy frame out of the door. "I'm sure he's amenable to reason."

They watched and waited until the door slowly opened, and the man in the blue overalls emerged. He looked right and left, to make sure that the coast was clear, then picked up his heavy sack and prepared to leave.

Then he saw Feathers. Josh couldn't make out what Feathers said to him, but he knew it involved the pistol which he held, pressed against the man's stomach. They were arguing about something. The man didn't appear keen to go back inside. Then Feathers pointed to the sack which the man refused to open. Then he heard a shot, followed by a howl of pain, as the man stared at his foot. He looked fearful now and fumbled around inside the sack until he retrieved the timepiece. He handed it to Feathers, who adjusted it.

That meant it was safe to go inside. They watched and waited as the man limped back into the house, followed by Feathers with his pistol thrust in the small of his back. Josh donned his necklace again to observe Feathers following the man round the kitchen, as he detached all the wiring and replaced it in his sack. At one point, Feathers made a phone call, with the phone in one hand and his pistol in the other. The precaution hardly seemed to matter now, as the man had become absorbed in the pain in his foot.

As Josh sat in the car and waited, a police car pulled in behind them and two officers emerged. One of them peered through their window and said, "If you wait a bit, while we check the premises, it should be safe to go in." They emerged a few minutes later. bundled the man in blue overalls into their car and drove off.

Everyone entered the house and moved into the kitchen. Feathers bustled around, getting everyone seated and pouring out drinks.

"I don't understand," said Megs. "I thought those drones had been banned."

"In theory, yes," said Josh's dad, "but I expect there are a few hidden away."

"The Prince ordered a new batch," said Prunella. "He gets them from my stepmother in Neustria. He told me lots of stuff like that."

"And what did you say?" asked Feathers, observing her with amused curiosity.

"I said 'how wonderful!' of course. That's why I'm still alive."

Josh laughed and ran upstairs to place his necklace in the cupboard beside his bed. On the way down again, he heard a protest going on outside the kitchen window; shouts and the hooting of car horns and what sounded like rifle shots. The Prince had seized his moment, he thought. Any moment now, he imagined a group of his supporters breaking into the house. He saw his dad follow Feathers outside to investigate. Then, from further away, on the other side of the house, he faintly heard the drone of an approaching helicopter. The last sound he heard was a "Wait for me!" from Megs as he ran into the lounge and opened the French windows to investigate.

The moment he stepped into the garden, a massive blow on the side of his head brought him to his knees and, while he struggled to regain consciousness, he felt strong arms on either side dragging him stumbling across the grass and up the slope beyond the grass towards the deafening roar of the helicopter touching down a few feet from where he stood.

Propped up by the two masked men who towered over him, he felt that help lay close at hand, but utterly beyond his reach. He watched the small, triumphant figure of Ronald Fleck remove his helmet and goggles as he stepped down from the helicopter. "Well. This is a nice surprise!" said Fleck, nodding to the masked men. "I see you're all bundled up and ready to go," he said to Josh, with a leer of satisfaction. "I'm taking you to see the Prince. I warned you, but would you listen? This is your reward for all the lies you've been spreading about him."

Josh closed his eyes. His head throbbed with pain, and he couldn't move, his arms pinned in place by the strength of those muscled men. His parents and friends couldn't help. They had gone to deal with the riot on the other side of the house. He felt himself being dragged like a sack towards the helicopter.

Then the man on his left suddenly released his grip. Josh opened his eyes to find him lying flat on the ground with an arrow in his back. Seconds later, the man on his right jerked forward and lurched headfirst to the ground, too. In a sudden ecstasy of hope, Josh felt free to move. But Fleck stood only a few feet away from him, and he held a pistol in his hand.

Then a prim voice from the edge of the garden called out, "I wouldn't do that if I were you, because my arrow will reach you first."

Fleck hesitated. "How can I be sure you won't shoot?" he said, pointing his pistol hands down.

"You can't," said Prunella, and shot the arrow straight into his chest.

"All's fair in love and war," she said, stooping in front of Fleck's body to pick up his pistol. "Archery's my favourite sport," she explained, "but I haven't practised it on people before. I don't think I'd like to do it again, but I didn't mind doing it to him."

"You saved my life," said Josh.

"Yes, probably," said Prunella. "He should have shot straight away. Bullets fly faster than arrows. Are you well enough to walk?"

Josh nodded.

"Thanks," he said, as he followed her back through the garden.

As soon as he reached the safety of the lounge, Josh just lay back on the sofa and listened to the voices in the background as if they came from a different world; voices of concern from his mum and Megs, giving him pills to swallow and applying cold compresses to the bump on the side of his head, and voices from his dad and Feathers talking about police protection and safety. He couldn't go anywhere now, he thought. The idea of being housebound for ever weighed on his mind.

"It's your necklace that's having that effect on you," said his mum, observing his reaction. "I'm told it's much more powerful than the single stone you used to wear. It's vitally important, for your safety as much as anything, but you can't use it too often."

"But I don't understand," said Megs. "You can't expect Josh to sit around all day, doing nothing. If the necklace is so powerful, isn't there some way he could use it to get back at the Prince?"

"In what way, Megs?"

"Well, you saw how he was able to release all those men from their barges. Couldn't he use those powers to attack the Prince directly?"

"That's different, Megs," said Josh's mum. The necklace can be used to save lives, but not to kill people. There are two lives at stake now. The Prince will have Prunella in his sights, too. But, so long as we ask the police to vet arrivals, and so long as Josh checks his necklace every time one of you leaves the house, you should all be safe.

"I have asked the police to come and remove the bodies," said Feathers, when he returned to the lounge. "They have agreed to keep a 24- hour watch on the house until the crisis is over."

"Are they watching the sky?" asked Prunella. "That's where the next attack will come from."

Feathers nodded. "I'll make another phone call," he said.

After a short delay, a helicopter arrived and circled overhead for the rest of the night.

Josh stayed on in the lounge, talking with Megs and Prunella, long after his parents departed, and Feathers lumbered upstairs to bed. The two girls did most of the talking. Megs wanted to know about Neustria and Prue's time with the Prince, and who was worse – the Prince or her stepmother -and Prunella decided that the Prince was ahead in the badness stakes, but it was a close-run thing.

Josh sat locked in his thoughts. From time to time, Megs glanced in his direction and looked away again. He knew what she was thinking, and she finally said it. "We can't go on like this!" she said. "We can't really go off on shopping sprees together, while poor Josh sits around waiting to be killed. Anyway," she added. "I know you, Josh! You'd take a risk – and most of the time you'd get away with it. But the Prince would get you in the end. There must be some better solution!"

"There is another way," said Prue quietly. "We can go to Neustria."

Megs stared at her as if she were mad. "Then we'd all get killed!" she said.

"Neustria's a big place. It depends where we go," said Prue.

Josh thought of that girl at the chess table and the way she planned her moves. It was almost a miracle, he thought, the way she'd evaded her stepmother and the Prince. Perhaps this next move had been at the back of her mind all the time.

"I have a friend," she said. "Well. Not really a friend. He's an ally. He'll do anything for me if he thinks he'll get something in return. He's the governor of Terrestria. That's a province in the far south of my country. He was a great friend of my father's, too. His name's Bellagra. They don't like my stepmother in Terrestria."

"What about the Prince?" asked Megs.

"Nobody in Neustria likes the Prince," said Prue. "Close to Terrestria there must be about five thousand of your colonists, all wearing circlets, and slaving away in the fields. If you could free those colonists like you did with those bargemen, we'd have an army ready to march on the capital. The Terrestrians would join us, and other provinces would join us too as we marched north."

"Are you really sure of all this?" Josh asked.

"Oh yes," said Prunella. "You see, I'm popular in Neustria. Well, my father was popular, really, and people would generally prefer his daughter to succeed than some greedy woman who got there by killing her husband."

Josh and Megs exchanged glances. "Well, it's an idea," he said. "Let's talk about it in the morning with Feathers."

"Why do you need to talk to Feathers?" asked Prunella.

"Well, it needs planning."

"I've told you the plan," said Prunella.

## CHAPTER NINETEEN

Josh spent a sleepless night tossing Prunella's crazy plan around and around in his head. The Prince couldn't attack them in Neustria. And he wouldn't dare send agents there to assassinate them, either. And if they could muster an army – an army of five thousand colonists released from their circlets - that army could not only be useful to Prunella but could return to the Western Isles and help them overthrow the Prince. But how would they get there without being caught? And how would they get back with an army of that size? Who would provide the transport they needed? Would Bellagra help them? Would Prue persuade him to help them?

These questions were too big for him to answer. They would involve Feathers and his parents and the general and Jack Sands. But what if they said 'yes'? Well, they probably wouldn't say 'yes'. With these thoughts turning around and around in his mind, he finally fell asleep.

He got up late the next morning and ate breakfast in a deserted kitchen. The bump on the side of his head still felt sore and had given him a headache, but Prunella's plan had given him cause for hope.

Feathers strode into the kitchen and sat at the table. He leaned over and ruffled Josh's hair and took a close look at him. "Come on, Josh!"

he said. "Things are not that bad! It must be awful not being able to leave the house without someone trying to kill you. But the Prince is not going to win this war. We won't let him!"

"Prunella says we should go to Neustria," said Josh, not daring to look up from his plate.

Feathers came and sat at the table. To Josh's astonishment, he sounded quite positive about the idea. "Yes, they've been telling me about it," he said. "It has its merits. You'd be safe there. The main problem is how to get off this island – without being caught. I have a solution, but I'm not sure if you'll like it. It involves pretending to be sick. How do you fancy a short spell in the local hospital?"

Josh thought he didn't mind anything so long as it just meant pretending.

"I spoke with your parents last night," said Feathers. "And they agree that you can't go on as you are. So, any alternative, however crazy it seems, is better than what you are facing now. But what if the Prince thinks that you are ill – I mean really ill? If we can fool him into believing you're no longer a threat, we should be able to get you safely off these islands."

Josh remembered the last time he'd spent at the local hospital. That time he'd nearly died. This time sounded too easy. "How long would I have to stay in hospital?" he asked.

Feathers shrugged. "Not more than two or three days," he said.

"But what about Prunella? Isn't she at risk too?"

"We thought about that. We certainly can't let her wander out of the house where she would risk getting recaptured. But even her stepmother would be forced to react if a foreign Prince killed the Empress in waiting. The Prince knows that."

Once he'd agreed to the plan, Josh felt as useless as he'd felt at school when asked to play the corpse in a crime drama. He sat around in the lounge all morning, hearing Megs and Prunella chatting away, while Feathers hurried round the house, phoning his parents and the council in Elephantia. Then he listened to the news of his 'serious illness' on the local radio, which meant Feathers had to answer more calls- this time from islanders, hoping that 'the young Guardian' would soon make a speedy recovery. He thought more than once of putting on his necklace, to see if the Prince was listening, but decided he'd rather not know.

Then his parents arrived, and his mum came and sat beside him in the kitchen and tried to comfort him. "It's the best hope we have, dear." she said, with her arm round his shoulder. "Megs and Prue will be with you, and Feathers, of course. I couldn't sleep last night, worrying about those awful men trying to kill you. Once you get to Neustria, nobody can touch you."

This wasn't just about safety, Josh thought. Prunella's plan involved much more than that. It involved returning with an army. He thought Feathers realised that, but he was not sure if his mum did.

They listened to the news together and Josh learned to his relief that the resistance forces had just won a great victory in Crown Colony. The general's forces had advanced to within a few miles of Paradise City. "That will keep the Prince busy," said his mum. "The council decided to speed up our campaign. It's a diversion, if you like, to keep his eyes focussed elsewhere."

After his parents left, there was a loud knock at the door. Seconds later, a doctor and nurse hurried into the living room carrying a stretcher. They placed it on the living room floor. The nurse smiled, and asked him to lie on it. He discovered to his relief that no acting was involved, as everything took place inside the house. Megs and Prunella called "Good Luck!" and "See you soon!" A white sheet was placed over his body, and he was rushed out of the house and into a waiting ambulance.

He shut his eyes and listened to the blaring sound of the ambulance forcing its way through the traffic in the centre of town. Then he felt a sudden jolt, as it stopped. The doors swung open, and he found himself being lifted onto a trolley and conveyed through the warm air of a summer afternoon into the antiseptic atmosphere of a busy hospital, buzzing with the sound of nurses, doctors and their patients, all talking in low voices. A door opened and closed, and he felt himself ascending several floors in a lift, then rolled along a corridor and finally wheeled into a room and lifted onto a bed.

It was a large room for just one patient, containing a bed, a bedside table, and two chairs for visitors. There was a partition down the middle of the room, and a large man in police uniform appeared through the door in this partition and introduced himself as Gonzalez. "I'm here for your safety," he explained. "In case of suspicious visitors enquiring after your health. Now, we don't want that, do we? I am here to welcome them, as you might say."

Gonzalez grinned and held up a pair of handcuffs. Then he retired behind the partition and the doctor and nurse returned to the room and told him he was now free to move around. They would be notified by reception if he had visitors, so he had ample time to prepare for them. In the meantime, would he like anything to eat? Josh quickly agreed to the offer of food but explained that he'd be quite happy not to have any visitors at all. The doctor understood and informed reception that the patient was being held in quarantine, as his disease was highly contagious. From then on, he was free to read, listen to the radio, and play endless games of cards with the young nurse, whose name was Angie. Time passed very slowly.

His release came on the third day, soon after midnight, when the young nurse told him to get up and follow him down to reception. There he found an impatient Feathers, who clapped him on the shoulder and propelled him out of the hospital. Emerging from the brightly lit interior, he had trouble adjusting his eyes to the darkness of the night.

Feathers hurried him towards a battered grey van, with fishing tackle strapped to the roof, parked opposite the hospital. "Meet Andy!" said Feathers, pointing to the driver; a grey-haired man with a sharp pointy face and a ruddy complexion, whose van had a strong smell of fish. "Andy's here to take us to the island of Verania," he said. "It's just a short journey across the water."

His spirits rose as he sat beside Megs and Prunella in the back of the van and they drove downhill in the dark towards the harbour. It was cold inside the van, and nobody spoke much. Then Andy made a sudden left, and the van bumped down an unlighted dirt track which led through fields to a tiny inlet where his fishing dory was moored. The sea was flat that night and Andy reckoned that the crossing would be done in an hour.

Josh began to feel in his element now as he waded through the muddy water to the boat. He clambered on board first and reached down to help Megs and Prunella climb up and join him. Andy looked on, amused, then pointed to a ladder on the other side of the boat which he and Feathers used to climb on board. Andy sat at the tiller, started the engine, and they were off.

The girls had had enough by this stage. Megs whispered that they'd been cooped up in the house for three days, because of fears for Prunella's safety. They wanted to celebrate their first day of freedom. He could hear them laughing and chatting below decks in the cabin while he sat beside Andy at the tiller.

It was a warm night and Feathers removed his heavy overcoat, folded it into a bundle and sat on it, resting his back against the side of the cabin. "I can't tell you exactly where we're heading, after we reach Verania," he said. "There are a lot of little islands in the southern seas, and our choice depends on choosing a route where we are most likely to escape detection. Your necklace should help us there."

He unfolded a map and pushed it in Josh's direction. "I've marked our arrival point in Neustria," he said, as Josh reached over to take the map. "It's a small coastal town on the east coast called Havelock. Its chief advantage is that it's far from the capital, and it does have a lock – which means that it has a river. It also has a railway station and there is a small airport nearby. So we need to be heading east, but we can talk about that in the morning."

They had reached the island by now, which turned out to be no more than a barren strip of rock, two hundred yards long and about half that in width, with two huts containing beds and blankets and cooking equipment for passing fishermen. Megs and Prunella, still talking about their plans, hurried into one, while Josh and Feathers headed for the other. Andy preferred to sleep in his boat and was already busy laying nets for his morning catch.

# CHAPTER TWENTY

Josh knew that the boat journey across the water was bound to be the difficult bit. As he crawled out of his tent on the small island of Verania, the halfway point where they'd landed the night before, Josh wondered how long it would take for the Prince to learn of their intentions. It would take a few more hours to reach the coast of Neustria, but those few hours would be fraught with danger.

The others weren't up yet. He gulped down a glass of milk and wandered away from the camp to consult his necklace. He felt he was beginning to get the hang of it. As soon as he put it on, it seemed to respond to the word 'worry' – or, more likely, his actual concern. His view wandered eastward from the clear skies ahead to the larger islands on their route; some of them, he knew, were as large as Amaryllis. He saw helicopters circling the skies in that area. Did that mean anything?

Against his will, his thoughts were drawn to the Prince. He saw him clearly now, not on his yacht but striding along the street. He recognised that street; it was one of the main shopping streets in Crown Colony. But most of the shops were closed. Some were even boarded up. Only the Prince and his retinue walked that street. These were his trusted followers, rifles at the ready. None of them wore circlets. *Josh walked among them now, a shadow in their midst. The*

*Prince glanced left and right, quivering with fury. He'd grown fatter and coarser than that time when Josh met him in Windfree. Josh recognised Fernando, the man he was talking to, the tall dark-haired lieutenant from Windfree. "I tell you I've been tricked!" the Prince shouted. "That boy wasn't sick! I'll show him what sickness means! We have to search the southern seas and track him down before he gets to Neustria."*

*"And the girl?" asked Fernando.*

*"No," the Prince decided. "Her stepmother can deal with that girl. She's no use to us anymore." Then he gave a grim laugh and added, "Not that all of this matters! Crown Colony is ours now. By the time he returns, we'll have taken Elephantia and we'll be lords of the Western Isles!"*

Josh removed the necklace. The Prince's last words rang in his ears. He thought of all the people he knew, either captured or killed, or beating a retreat to Elephantia. He had to return with that army soon in order to make a difference! But he'd never seen the Prince lose control of himself before. He drew a small grain of comfort from what he'd seen. Losing his temper suggested that things might not be going entirely the Prince's way. He saw Feathers emerging from the hut and ran over to discuss what he'd learnt.

Josh hesitated. What could he learn from the necklace that would help them in their present situation? Alone, and miles from land, their little boat could be spotted by any passing helicopter. And that would be true for the next six hours at least.

Despite his worries, they were nearly in sight of shore before he spotted the first helicopter.

"The enemy aren't the only ones trying to find us!" Feathers shouted, keeping one hand on the tiller. "Do you imagine our friends would go to all that trouble arranging your escape, and then forget about you? They must be out there somewhere. For all we know, that helicopter's one of ours."

Josh banged his palm against his forehead in frustration at his stupidity. Of course, his parents and the council would be spending every waking minute worrying about the escape mission. He put on the necklace and thought about his parents. Nothing happened. They must be thinking about him. He knew that! But why couldn't he see them? Thinking about anybody else felt like a betrayal. It wouldn't work anyway, he thought.

"The necklace isn't working," he said.

Feathers struggled for an answer. He had enough on his hands, holding the boat on course while bumping through the ocean at maximum speed. "It must be working!" he said.

Prunella leaned against the wall of the cabin, listening to this exchange. "It wouldn't work in Neustria," she said.

"Come closer!" Feathers shouted. "I can't hear you!"

"I can't come any closer!" she shouted. "There's nothing to hold on to. I was just trying to say that, as you approach my country, the necklace will probably stop working. It was designed by pirates, a long time ago, according to the laws that govern the Western Isles." She shrugged. "I didn't expect it to work in this part of the world," she said.

Why hadn't she told him that before? Josh wondered. Without the power of the necklace, how could they possibly release those slaves? Wasn't that the whole point of the journey?

No time to think about that now, he thought. High up in the sky to the east, he saw something that sent a shiver through his veins - a tiny black speck descending in their direction. As he watched, it grew to the size of a bird, and then to something much larger. He could just make out its telltale drone, and that soon grew louder too. "A helicopter!" he shouted.

Feather had seen it too and started to steer an uneven course in a vain attempt to elude its threatening dive.

Then Josh spotted another black speck descending from the east. "There's two of them now!" he cried.

Within seconds, bullets pinged in the water all around the dory and Josh stood frozen in fear. Then a strange thing happened. Suddenly, out of nowhere, the helicopter burst into flames and tumbled through the air into the water barely fifty yards from where he stood. Josh quickly turned his attention to the second helicopter, diving in the direction of the dory. Within seconds, this helicopter too, came too close for comfort, but when it reached within shooting range, the pilot leant out of the cockpit and gave a friendly wave.

Josh watched in amazement as this second helicopter ascended into the skies. But instead of returning to the east, it stayed there like a tiny black spot to protect them on their voyage.

· · · ● ● · ● ● · ·

All that happened only yesterday, Josh thought, as he sat in the light aircraft, enjoying the way it dipped and swayed in the wind as it ate up the last miles of their journey to Belmondo. Prunella had done them proud. He admired the way she had handled the pilot, first forcing him to drive all the way to collect them from their landing place, then calmly haggling with him until they arrived at what she called an acceptable price for the journey. The poor chap seemed to accept it in good part, so she probably knew what she was doing.

He had been asleep for a while. Megs, in the seat behind, was chatting to Prunella. He heard her ask, "What do you think about Bellagra, Prue? Will he help us?"

"Well, he doesn't like my stepmother," said Prue.

Josh looked at Feathers in the window seat beside him. That wasn't the answer he wanted to hear. Feathers shrugged.

"I can see how that helps you, Prue," said Megs, "But it doesn't help us."

"Well, that necklace doesn't work in Neustria. That could be a problem."

"Yes, but you knew that, Prue. That's not good enough!"

Josh felt the tension in the plane mounting. He noticed Feathers had turned to look out of the window.

"I can ask him to imprison the men guarding those slaves," said Prunella. "I'd been planning to do that. Then I'm sure he can find the tools to release your five thousand men. I might even persuade him to arm them."

"Why didn't you say that before?"

"Because it may come at a cost. I don't know what he may want of me in return."

Josh suspected that she did know, but didn't want to say. An important person like Bellagra – maybe he wanted the empire for himself. He realised why she'd been keeping so quiet.

Josh kept thinking about what Prunella had said earlier. Bellagra was an ally; not exactly a friend. She wanted his help, but the price he was asking might be more than she wanted to pay. Somehow, she'd find a way round it, he decided. With this comforting thought, he shut his eyes and dozed off to sleep again.

He woke up, terrified that he was falling off a cliff, then remembered that he was on a plane, making a bumpy descent from high altitude. Then he heard Megs chatting with Prunella in the seat in front. They hadn't talked like that since they left the bungalow in Amaryllis. The sound cheered him. He knew Megs wouldn't be talking to her like that if she didn't trust her.

He tried to imagine what it would be like meeting Bellagra. It sounded like a pirate name.

He imagined a tall man, with black hair and a prominent nose, who would greet them with a bit of a flourish and welcome Prunella like a doting uncle. Perhaps he meant to hide his ambitions until he'd placed her on the throne and then do what her stepmother had done; pull all the strings and treat her as a puppet. Prunella wouldn't stand for that!

Megs' face appeared, peering at him from the seat in front. "Wake up, Josh," she said. "We're passing over Terrestria now."

He saw that they were descending over a mountain range. The downward slope flattened into a range of rocky outcrops and, beyond that, he could just make out a fertile valley full of vineyards and orchards. As the plane descended, he saw a river running through the valley, and a bridge with red-roofed houses clustered on either side. He could even see people now, and cars, and finally, in the distance, the outskirts of the city itself. "That's Belmondo," said Prunella, leaning over the back of her seat to talk to him. "It used to be the capital of Neustria. Some of the palaces and temples are over a thousand years old. They built in marble in those days."

Josh could see the whole city now, laid out before its eyes, with its river and its gardens, its courtyards, and its palaces. He thought it was the most beautiful city he'd ever seen.

## CHAPTER TWENTY-ONE

At the back of the Arrivals Hall, Josh saw a large man in an open tweed jacket, with straw hair sprouting in all directions and a red tie dangling over his belly, laughing and chatting with a small group of important-looking men and women in smart clothes. Prunella waved to the man, and he raised an arm to greet her.

"Who's that?" Josh whispered in Prunella's ear.

"Didn't I tell you?" whispered Prunella, growing a little pink with embarrassment. "That's Count Bellagra. I phoned him as soon as we arrived, so he must have hurried to get here. He's very popular in Belmondo at the moment. They say he's frightfully intelligent, and he's promised to do all sorts of wonderful things for our region." She smiled and waved at him, and he returned her greeting.

Bellagra wasn't at all as Josh had imagined. He looked more like a celebrity than a political leader. But he radiated an infectious energy. This was a man who would get things done.

A small man with a nervous face like a rabbit stood at his shoulder. His anxious eyes darted around the hall.

"We're going to make Belmondo great again!" Bellagra said, to cheers from his admirers. "We're going to build a railway all the way to the capital of Neustria!"

Josh heard the small man whisper in Bellagra's ear, "We've already got one."

"Yes, but we're going to massively improve it!" Bellagra said, to more cheers from his admirers. Josh thought that he didn't seem to mind being corrected, and his admirers didn't seem to mind, either. He had a cheeky smile on his face which suggested that he might make the odd mistake but, with a chap like himself in charge, it would all come out right in the end. Bellagra gave them a friendly wave and strode over to greet Prunella. He threw his thick arms around her and cried, "Welcome to Belmondo!". Then he said, loud enough for his followers to hear, "Beautiful as ever! I have known this young lady since she was a baby in her mother's arms. Welcome to the future Empress of Neustria!"

His followers clapped and cheered, but Prunella whispered in Josh's ear, "He likes to exaggerate a bit. That's his way!"

Bellagra shook Feathers by the hand, greeting him as 'the famous explorer from the Western Isles.' Then it was Meg's turn. He held on to her hand a little bit longer and pronounced her 'the poster Queen of Amaryllis.' Then Josh, 'the Pirate Guardian with magical powers.' Josh had a fleeting impression of a friendly face and a jokey manner, and blue eyes that gazed beyond him into the secret space of his ambitions.

"We'll go on a boat," said Bellagra. "Yes, that's what we'll do! We'll go on a boat. What better way to show you the wonders of Belmondo?"

"The boat's waiting at the Septimal Bridge," said the rabbit face.

"That's his adviser," whispered Prunella. "His real name is William, but people call him 'the wizard.'"

Outside the airport, Bellagra's entourage dispersed. Feathers had a quick word with the wizard, and a taxi arrived to take their baggage to a small hotel next to Bellagra's palace. Then Bellagra and his wizard led them along the pavement and down a side road which led to the river.

Within minutes of leaving the airport, they found themselves reclining on a gondola, lazily enjoying the river smells, and the sound of the lapping water and the sight of palaces and museums and colleges gliding by, with their lawns and gardens stretching down to the river's edge.

Bellagra and the wizard sat opposite, with their backs to the direction in which they were heading. Josh noticed that Bellagra had stopped talking and seemed content to sit and smile, giving an occasional yawn, like a lion relaxing before his next encounter. He seemed capable of enormous spurts of energy, driving his plans forward but, in the meantime, he seemed content to chat and listen.

It was the wizard who did the talking. "I gather you are here on a mission," he said in a high, precise voice. "We would be interested to hear about that."

Prunella spoke first. "My stepmother has stolen my empire," she said. "I am here to reclaim it."

The wizard raised his eyebrows in alarm. "Your stepmother is very powerful," he began. "And in some quarters, she is still quite popular."

"She killed my father. Not everyone knows that."

The wizard shrugged. "Well, I can't say that anyone knows that for sure," he said. "I understand he was stung by a bee."

"An artificial bee! A drone. If people knew that, I don't think she would be popular at all."

Feathers cleared his throat and said, "The evidence of other drone attacks on important citizens makes it clear that he was murdered."

The wizard nodded. "I must confess I have heard as much," he added. He turned to Prunella. "Neustria would be a better place if you were Empress," he said. "The question is what you want us to do about it."

Josh noticed that Bellagra still said nothing. He just sat there and smiled at Prunella as if to say, *It's up to you to make your case. You had better make it a good one.* Josh knew that if he didn't speak soon, his mission would fail. He turned to Bellagra, and asked, as if in a casual quest for information, "Is it true that you support slavery?"

The wizard stole an anxious glance at his master, but Bellagra had already risen to the bait. "Slavery!" he exclaimed, sitting bolt upright and waving his great arms in the air, "is the most rotten form of exploitation ever devised by the human race! Of course, I don't support slavery!"

"I hoped you'd say that," said Josh, "because there are five thousand colonists from the Western Isles working as slaves on your estates. Are you happy about that?"

"It's a shocking state of affairs!" said Bellagra. "It should be stopped!"

The wizard whispered a few words in his ear, and Bellagra added "I mean, in an ideal world it should be stopped."

"But you have the power to stop it now," said Josh. "All you have to do is arrest their masters and seize their controls and five thousand colonists will be released."

Bellagra's eyes shifted uncomfortably from Josh to Prunella, and then to the wizard at his side.

Josh tried a different approach. "Are the people of Terrestria happy to lose their jobs to five thousand foreigners doing the same work for free?"

Josh noticed the wizard's anxious eyes focus on his master, who opened and closed his mouth like a bullfrog in his eagerness to express his noble intentions. "What do you want with these slaves?" he asked.

"We want what they want," said Josh, "to be free to return to their own lands and to help us in our war against the Rebel Prince."

The wizard nibbled his lips and stared into space. Then he turned to Bellagra and said, "Well, it would make you very popular."

Bellagra could contain himself no longer. "Let's do it now," he said. "Let's do it in time for the evening news. We can free those slaves. We can arm them. We can send them on a train to the capital. With the help of our troops, they can topple that terrible regime."

"We don't have any troops," said the wizard.

Bellagra glared and his hands began to shake as if he had a sudden urge to place them round the wizard's throat. "What do you mean?" he spluttered. "We have thousands of troops."

"We have thousands of guns," said the wizard, "but we only have *two hundred* soldiers. If you recall, we were forced to disband our army on direct orders from the capital."

In a sudden change of tack, Bellagra turned to Prunella. "Well, we will help you anyway," he said. "It's a shocking situation. We will free those slaves and we will arm them. Those troops will install you as Empress. I'll help you with that. It's the least I can do."

"Yes, thanks very much," said Prunella.

Bellagra turned to the wizard. "How far is it to those fields?" he asked. "The fields where those poor slaves are toiling away in the sun? An hour's train journey, perhaps?"

The wizard nodded.

"Well, send those troops you mentioned on the next train, have the slave masters arrested and disarmed, and send the slaves to the armoury to have their helmets removed and to be re-equipped with rifles and so forth. I want this all to be done in time for the evening news."

The wizard gulped and gave a little shake of his head.

Bellagra placed an arm over his shoulder. "Can you do that?" he asked.

The wizard looked over his shoulder and winced. "I can try," he said.

"Good," said Bellagra. "And now I would like a little word with my darling, Prunella."

"What did he say?" asked Josh, as they stepped off the gondola, and her whispered conversation with Bellagra was over.

"He offered to help me install the new government," said Prunella. "I was expecting that."

"That's good, isn't it?" said Megs. "His help could be useful. What did you say?"

"I thanked him, of course," said Prunella. "Well, I had to say something," she added.

# CHAPTER TWENTY-TWO

At half-past nine that evening, they watched Bellagra's smiling face on television announce to the cheering crowds that he had just released five thousand slaves from the Western Isles and intended to return them to their homes. Then Josh and his companions checked out of the hotel that had been booked for them that very morning and headed for the station. As soon as they stepped onto the platform, they were cheered by a long line of emaciated soldiers clad in army fatigues and armed with rifles.

"How do you like our soldiers" asked Bellagra, placing an arm over William the Wizard. "A fine body of men, don't you think?"

"I think they look hungry," said Prunella, frowning. "And they are not our soldiers."

Josh noticed that Bellagra didn't seem to be listening.

"They need food," the wizard agreed, "but in modest amounts at first. It will take time for their bodies to recover."

"Yes, yes, modest amounts," said Bellagra, patting his stomach. He pointed at the train, with its long line of coaches stretching a long way behind the point where Josh and his companions were standing. "Virtually every coach is a buffet car! William and I have been up all night - haven't we, William? – to ensure that every coach is loaded with provisions. Enough to feed an army, I'd say."

"Yes, well, it is an army," said William the Wizard, with the glazed stare of an overworked official.

At that moment, amid cheers from the troops, the freshly elected leader of that army stepped forward and shook hands with the little group gathered round Bellagra. He had a broad chest and a prominent belly, no mean accomplishment in the light of his recent captivity, and a stern, weathered face with a glint of dour humour in his dark eyes. He was, by his own admission, 'a simple butcher from Colony Island,' but Josh remembered that he had made a name for himself in the war against Reginald Machin.

"I'm Ed Smith," he said, in a plain-speaking sort of voice. "I've had a bit of experience of warfare. That's why the men have voted me in as their commander." He gave a cheerful grin. "Leastwise, we all know what we have to do; install the young Empress on her throne and then move on to Elephantia and fight to overthrow the Prince. Now, if you don't mind, I'll order my men to board the train and get stuck in to all that food you've so generously provided. Whoever organised that at such short notice, I take my hat off to him. He must be a wizard!"

Josh smiled to himself. He wondered if Ed Smith had guessed that his army owed a lot to William the Wizard.

The journey to the capital of Neustria lasted most of the night. Josh sat with Feathers and Megs and Prunella in an empty compartment at the rear of the train, listening to the cheers and the clink of cutlery of five thousand soldiers celebrating their newfound freedom.

Josh sat by the window, wrapped in his thoughts, wondering what would happen when they arrived at the capital. Would it really be so easy to install Prunella on her throne? And then, how would they manage to convey this vast number of soldiers to Elephantia? He glanced at Prunella. She looked calm enough. And Feather had already managed to fall asleep. Megs sat beside him. She patted him on the arm. "Don't worry, Josh," she said. "What happens next is beyond our control."

Halfway through the night, Josh heard a tap on the door of the carriage and Prunella excused herself. Josh saw her standing in the corridor, having a whispered conversation with William the Wizard. Feathers woke up and muttered, "This looks interesting." He got up and left the carriage to join them.

Josh felt an immediate sense of relief. If William and Feathers were involved in this, he sensed that there was a plan that might actually work. He glanced at Megs, who whispered, "I could tell from Prue's face that something was afoot."

Josh saw the three figures in the corridor talking and nodding. They finally shook hands and filed back into the carriage.

"Bellagra has fallen asleep," William explained, once they were all seated. "So I thought this might be a suitable moment for me to offer my services to the Empress."

Prunella gave a secretive smile. "William has been giving me some useful advice," she said.

"Well, we all want an orderly transition, don't we?" said the wizard, appealing to Feathers.

"More to the point, we need you," said Feathers.

Just then, the train slowed down and jerked to a halt. The voice of Bellagra boomed over the microphone installed in each carriage. "I am sorry about this slight delay, chaps," the voice announced, "but we will soon be arriving at the capital. I am, of course, determined to ensure an orderly change of government, with no bloodshed of course, and that's why I have taken this moment to let you all know that I have decided to take on the demanding role of commander-in-chief. I intend to—"

At that moment, Josh saw the wizard press a little button on his phone and the speech was cut off. At the same time, he glanced at Feathers, who got up and left the carriage. Josh saw him striding down the corridor. "What was all that about?" he asked.

"I always thought Bellagra would do something like this," said Prunella.

"Then why didn't you stop him?"

"I wanted to, but William thought—"

"I thought it would be better to let him say enough to incriminate himself," said William. "Otherwise, who knows? Some of those soldiers might have supported him." He stared at the floor and added, "Well, I must admit that I helped him record his speech, but I didn't feel we needed to hear all of it."

"You did the right thing!" said Megs. "By the way, what's Feathers doing now?"

"He's explaining everything to the soldiers," said William. "I removed Bellagra's phone and left him locked in the carriage. He'll have to stay like that until the Empress is safely installed on her throne. Otherwise, he could switch sides and warn her of our intentions."

Josh sat back and relaxed as the train got underway again. He didn't know what the future held, but he knew he was not involved in this part of it.

At four o'clock in the morning, it drew up at an empty station and the troops disembarked in silence. He and Megs lagged behind as casual spectators, observing Ed Smith and his five thousand men, fortified by their recent release and their first square meal, march through the deserted streets. A few bystanders opened their windows and watched in awe. When they spotted Prunella at the back of the line, escorted by Feathers and William the wizard, they waved and cheered.

Their arrival in the capital proved to be a bit of an anti-climax. The troops reached the imperial palace shortly before dawn. Josh saw Prunella's stepmother and her sister, shaken and protesting, and still in their nightclothes, being led away to prison. Then, with the help of Feathers and a small team of soldiers, Ed Smith made a lightning tour of the palace bedrooms, removing the occupants from their beds and informing them that, under the new government, they would have to look elsewhere for employment.

Feathers bustled around, offering to announce the glad tidings to the Neustrian people on the early morning news. The wizard bobbed up and down at his shoulder, pointing him in the direction of the newsroom.

Prunella waved and walked off to join Josh and Megs at a round table on the veranda overlooking the sea. They sat and watched the soldiers hurrying to and fro, conducting former government officials to their temporary accommodation in the town gaol. In the distance, they could just see the Neustrian battleship which Prunella, in her first command as Empress, had ordered to be loaned to the colonist army.

"There's your ship," said Prunella with pride. "My coronation will be tomorrow, but you'll miss that, I suppose."

"We'll miss you too," said Megs.

"You know that Feathers is staying behind to help me?" said Prunella.

Josh looked at Megs. The news took them both by surprise. But Josh felt pleased by the decision. Feathers was just the man she needed to help her select people she could trust to run her empire.

Out to sea, the battleship lay waiting and soldiers were already filing on board. Megs and Priscilla stood up, hugged each other, promised to stay in touch, and said their tearful goodbyes. Josh gave Priscilla a hug too and said he would always think of her as the girl, who was not only clever enough to beat the Prince at a game of chess but outsmarted him by pretending to lose.

# CHAPTER TWENTY-THREE

J osh and Megs stood at the ship's rail looking out for the first sight of Elephantia. They had a lot to talk about as the battleship wove its way through the smaller islands north of Amaryllis and out into the vast ocean beyond. Josh talked about Prunella, and how difficult it would be for a person of that age to run an empire. But Megs said that her friend, Prue, knew perfectly well that she wasn't running anything. She just had to be popular and have good people around her to make the decisions, and Feathers and William the Wizard would help her with that. The chief danger would come from another ambitious leader like Bellagra. But Prue had a ruthless streak – they both agreed about that - and Josh thought if she could handle such a man the way she'd handled the Prince, he'd soon find he'd taken on more than he could manage.

Then their thoughts turned to home and how they hated the idea of parting with Feathers. Josh hoped that Feathers would return soon, but Megs thought that unlikely to happen. He would want to stay on and see things through. Feathers was a great believer in 'seeing things through.' Anyway, when they got to Amaryllis, they'd find Josh's parents back in the bungalow. That was something to look forward to!

But they weren't heading for Amaryllis now! In fact, they'd already moved beyond the southern seas. An uncertain future lay ahead of them. "How long have we been away?" asked Josh, counting the days on his fingers.

Megs got there first. "Four days," she said, "if you count today." Then she added, "Go on. Josh! Put on that necklace!"

Josh had been postponing the moment as long as he dared. He wanted to see the good news first, so he put on the necklace and thought of his parents. *There they were, just as he'd imagined, eating lunch in the garden of the bungalow! His stepdad held a newspaper in his lap and was reading from it. "He was a good man." he said. "One of the best generals we ever had."*

*"How did he die?" asked his mum, bending forward to wipe the tears from her eyes. Josh hadn't seen his mum cry very often.*

*"In the final defence of Crown Colony. He died protecting our withdrawal. It's only thanks to General Fairbones, that the remainder of our army has been able to make a safe landing in Elephantia."*

Josh removed the necklace. He didn't want to learn any more.

"Why are you crying?" asked Megs. "I can't remember seeing you cry before."

"General Fairbones is dead."

And then Megs started crying too. "He was a good man," she sobbed.

Josh remembered how General Fairbones had kept their spirits up when they were all in imminent danger from the forces of Reginald Machin. "He never raised his voice," he said, "but everyone listened when he spoke. And he could be funny too."

"I was a bit stubborn and silly then," said Megs. "But he always took the trouble to listen to me." She dried her eyes as she saw Ed Smith heading in their direction across the deck.

"I need your help here," said Ed, turning to Josh. "We'll be landing in the capital of Elephantia soon, but I've no idea what we'll be up against. I believe you have the guardian's necklace, so you can see what nobody else can see – the exact disposition of the enemy forces and where our allies are at this moment in time."

Josh put on the necklace again.

His eyes wandered up and down the harbour and the quayside. Some of the buildings looked damaged, and he noticed a few windows that had been boarded up. But he saw very few people about; just a few residents peering from upstairs windows or hanging in doorways. The enemy seemed to be scattered in a long line, about a mile inland. Some of them wore circlets. He couldn't hear any firing, so the allies must be some distance away, on the outskirts of town. He remembered Jack Sands saying that the town was a no-go area, and that was some time ago. So it made sense that his forces would be waiting on the periphery.

He put away the necklace and reported what he'd seen to Ed Smith. Ed thanked him and invited Josh and Megs to follow him below deck, where the soldiers were gathered.

There was a hush as Ed stepped on to a table to address the troops. "We will shortly be landing in Newport," he said. "I have learned on good advice," he pointed to Josh, "that the enemy has advanced about a mile inland through the city. But their heads aren't pointing in our direction because they don't know we're here yet. They are advancing to do battle with our allies, who are waiting on the outskirts of town. Now, my watchword," he said, "is caution. I'm a great fan of not getting killed. As I say, they don't know we're here, so let's keep it that way as long as we can. As soon as we land in Newport, we will fan out over the whole area, and we'll move forward very slowly, keeping pace with one another. There's no point in hurrying. Let's take them by surprise. And watch out for those men wearing helmets. They may be on our side."

"How will we know?" asked a soldier.

"Good point," said Ed. "We won't. We'll just have to use our judgement. Now, there's a young chap here I want you all to meet. Some of you may already know him. He's the young Pirate Guardian. He was there on Colony Island when he used that stone thing of his to get rid of Reginald Machin. Well, he's got the whole necklace now. And you know what? He's already used that necklace to free two thousand colonists heading for the same fate as we suffered in the fields of Terrestria. Step forward, Josh and introduce yourself."

Josh took Ed Smith's outstretched hand and pulled himself up onto the table. He held up the necklace for the men to see, and said, "I have no idea how this thing works. I can only tell you what I see. The enemy have their backs to us. They are advancing through the town to meet the army of Elephantia. They are patrolling the streets, hiding in doorways. Some of them are wearing helmets. Their masters are generally standing behind them with those little black discs in their hands. Those are the ones you need to watch out for. Another thing you need to know is that some of their soldiers are armed with drones! You know those little metallic things that they used – or tried to use – to fertilise our crops? They're deadly, those drones. So, if you see anyone looking in your direction and fiddling with a little viewer thing, shoot him before he shoots you. That's all I can tell you."

"Do the enemy outnumber us?" asked one soldier.

"It looks like it," said Josh, "But they are marching to meet another enemy defending their own lands. That should give us an advantage."

"How did I do?" he asked Megs, stepping down from the table.

"I thought it was a good speech," said Megs. "You sounded very natural, and I liked that. You reminded me of John Bosworthy." She leaned forward and kissed him on both cheeks. "Now tell me the truth," she said, with a twinkle in her eyes. "Do they outnumber us?"

"Massively," he said.

"That's what I thought," she said. "Come on! It sounds as if the ship has landed. Let's follow them out on deck."

As the troops disembarked and spread out along the coastal highway, Ed followed along behind with Josh and Megs. "I need you both here beside me," he said. "Josh, you are my eyes and ears and--" he looked at Megs, "--you are the voice of common sense. I remember you from way back. I hope you haven't lost some of your mischief."

"She hasn't," said Josh.

"Good to hear it," said Ed. He pointed to a land rover parked on the other side of the road. "Now that little number should suit our purposes quite well. Is either of you any good at breaking into cars?"

"No need," said Megs. "The driver's door is open."

Ed gave a satisfied nod and turned to Josh. "The voice of common sense," he said.

Megs sat beside Ed upfront, while Josh sat in the back with the necklace.

"Could you disable those gadgets that control the helmets?" asked Ed.

"I could but it's not worth it!" said Josh. "It only takes one commander to press the destruct button and two hundred men get killed."

"Well, it might be worth the risk."

"Hardly," said Josh, removing the necklace. "I've watched those slaves in action. They either shoot to miss, or fire on their own commanders."

"Yeah, that's what I'd do too." said Ed. "Have they got many soldiers?"

"Real soldiers? The ones without helmets, you mean? It's hard to tell. All I can say is that every time I spot one of ours, I can see four or five of them. Mind you, they've mainly got their backs to us. They're fighting the enemy in front. Most of them haven't noticed us yet."

The only sound of fighting seemed to be coming from a long way ahead, on the northern outskirts of the town.

"We'd better start moving forward a bit, then," said Ed, starting the engine. He drove slowly, with the windows open, down the main avenue that cut through the centre of town. The soldiers from Neustria on either side of the avenue had advanced a few hundred yards, keeping close contact with each other and checking every street corner before waving one another forward. The enemy up ahead seemed unaware of their presence. Their fire was concentrated on the troops from the north.

Josh kept the necklace on. He could just make out 'the Terrestrians', as the freed army of colonists had mockingly decided to call themselves. They were advancing more rapidly now. They had reached the centre of the town, still hiding at every street corner, keeping pace with their comrades, and standing ready to provide covering fire when one of them crossed into the open. But the main sound of gunfire still seemed to be coming from a long way ahead, which meant that the enemy were advancing, and the allies were retreating. The Terrestrians had to get a move on. He passed the information to Ed.

Ed drove on until he reached the two Terrestrians on either side of the avenue. He beckoned them over and said, "Tell the men to surge forward and start firing."

Josh stepped out of the land rover and put on the necklace again. Megs came and stood by his side. He noticed that their allies had retreated to the outskirts of town now. He could see the backs of the enemy soldiers gathered in a thick mass at the end of central avenue.

The allied troops facing them looked pitifully few. They had parked an army lorry across the road and a few soldiers stood behind it, firing at intervals. He looked right and left along the allied line, scattered for more than a mile on either side of the avenue, and his heart sank. Men were falling, even as he watched. They couldn't hold out much longer, he thought.

Then he saw the trench. Behind the lorry, and all along their line, the allies had built a massive trench. That would have taken some time to prepare, he thought. They must have always known that the enemy would arrive by sea and capture the town, so they'd made very little effort to defend it. Instead, they'd built this trench, packed it with most of their army and lured the enemy towards it. Very few allied soldiers were visible now. They had all retreated to the trench.

He told Megs what he had seen, and she ran back to the land rover to report the news to Ed. The Terrestrians had begun to open fire now. All along the line, he could see the enemy turning back to face the unexpected threat from behind. And that's when the men in the trenches opened fire. Megs stood behind him again and tugged excitedly at his shoulder. "What's happening now?" she asked.

"We're winning!" Josh cried. "The enemy are facing heavy fire from both sides. If they don't surrender soon, it will turn into a massacre."

Ed got out of the land rover and joined them. "I heard you shouting," he said. "What's happening."

"We're winning!" he repeated. "The enemy are being fired at from both sides. They can't hold out much longer."

"Can you wait for me here?" asked Ed. "I'd better go and join my lads. I'll be back in a bit." He climbed back into the land rover and drove off.

## Chapter Twenty-Four

J osh stole a last look at his necklace. "It's finished!" he cried. "The enemy are laying down their rifles!" He turned to Megs and said, "I can't believe it! This wretched war will soon be over!"

"Are you sure?"

"It's chaos! Some of the enemy are still firing, but our Terrestrians are surging forward all along the line, driving them towards our friends in the trenches."

"Oh!" she said, giving him a hug. "What about the Prince?"

"I can't see him at the moment," he said. "Perhaps that's because I don't want to see him. Hey, Megs. What's the matter?"

At that moment, he felt her arms go limp and, before he could stop her, she dropped to the ground. Out of the corner of his eye, he saw the tall man with the drone disappear up a side street.

He looked at Megs lying there and suddenly, everything in his life became meaningless. Sobbing, he bent down, placed his hands under her fallen body, and kissed her on the lips. "I love you, Megs," he whispered. "You can't just die like that."

This person, who'd stood so close to him that he'd stupidly forgotten what she meant to him, had suddenly gone from him. Just like that. He thought of Lucy and how he'd been powerless to help her. But he hadn't got the necklace then. He clung to the hope that this might make a difference. He located the sting on the left side of her neck, removed it, and gently rubbed the place where it had landed. He felt her heart still beating. But her body lay inert, not exactly dead but lost to the world.

He stroked the side of her neck where the dart had gone in. She lay there like a statue, utterly beyond his reach. He dimly remembered being lost in that world himself once, when he'd been poisoned. He recalled how Megs had tried to revive him with the two stones in their possession. He'd at least felt her presence then, though he hadn't truly recovered until they'd found the medicine that cured him. Why couldn't he make her feel his presence now, as she'd once done for him? He fingered each stone in turn, the stone of truth which he'd originally possessed, the stone of knowledge which that man had stolen, and Lucy's stone – the most important stone of all.

He fingered the stone of love, and it glowed and grew warm to the touch. From somewhere deep in his heart, like water from a hidden spring, he felt the sudden upwelling of a love he'd never truly experienced before - the love of a friend that he'd so long taken for granted. "I love you, Megs," he said, stroking her temples with the stone of love. "Please don't die!"

To his sudden joy, he felt her tremble a little, as if a slight memory of life had returned to her. He clung to that thread of hope and willed that poison away, feeling it evaporate to a point where that tiny red mark on her skin had gone away. He raised her a little from the ground and felt a little warmth return to her body. Then, like a gift from the gods, she gave a little shudder and sat up.

"Where am I?" she asked, staring around her. "I can't remember where I've been."

"It doesn't matter," he said, helping her to her feet. He kept hold of her until he knew she'd recovered her balance. "You're safe now," he said.

"Is the war over?" she asked, still clinging on to him.

"I don't know. I think so," he said. "The Prince's army in Elephantia has been defeated. So, we'll soon be free to go back to our bungalow in Amaryllis."

"Oh, let's do that soon," she sighed. Then she glanced over her shoulder and gasped, "Look out! He's come back!"

The tall man with the drone had returned, except this time he carried a rifle. He wore a white robe, fringed with purple, and said in a casual voice. "I heard the young lady enquire if the war was over. Well, I still have my select band of loyal followers, and we will soon be retiring to Windfree, to regather our strength after a long campaign. Before I leave, I've decided to make you an offer."

"We're listening," said Josh.

"If you do what I ask, I won't try to kill you again, so you needn't be afraid."

"How do we know you are telling the truth?" asked Josh. "You killed your own brother, didn't you?"

The Prince paused to consider the question. "I did that for a reason," he said. "I could kill you too – or I could kill Megs first, and then I could kill you. But what are you, without the necklace? A harmless boy of average intelligence – a brave boy, admittedly, but one whose death would add no value to my campaign and might, in fact, make me unpopular in some quarters."

"You're already unpopular," said Megs. "Where is your select band? I believe they've deserted you."

"I'll forget you said that," the Prince replied in an even tone. "You see, all I want is that necklace."

"It won't be any use to you," said Josh.

"True," said the Prince, "but it will stop being useful to you, so I suggest you hand it over." He pointed his rifle at Megs.

She held Josh's hand even tighter. "Don't listen to him!" she urged him.

But Josh did listen. He removed his necklace, walked forward, and handed it to the Prince.

The Prince smiled and placed it over his head.

Then an extraordinary thing happened. The Prince groaned and dropped his rifle. He opened his mouth to protest, but no sound came out. His face went red, then darkened. The skin around his neck began to blacken and steam, and the blackness began to spread over the whole of his body. Then his body crashed to the ground and began to disintegrate and bubble, first like a rotting carcass and then like a thick length of tarred rope. Finally, his head collapsed into a molten, disfigured shape. And the shape grew smaller and solidified into the head of a snake. His arms and legs had already collapsed by this stage and formed his elongated tail. The black snake lingered on the pavement for a moment and lifted its head in their direction as if it had something to say. Then it just gave a hiss and slid away out of sight, condemned to restart its life at the lowest point on the ladder of creation.

Only the necklace remained on the ground, pure and untarnished. Josh stepped forward and picked it up.

Josh and Megs stared in wonder at the spot where the Prince had vanished from their world. They heard shouts and cheers in the distance, and the sound of marching feet heading in their direction, as the victorious allied armies led their hapless prisoners down the central avenue towards the harbour. They thought of the good people they had known whose lives had been thrown away, to satisfy the senseless ambitions of the Prince; the loving and innocent Sophie, the wise general Fairbones and all those men in helmets who'd died for a cause they didn't believe in.

Josh knew that his part in the story had ended and that the most valuable thing he had learned was that the girl standing beside him was his best friend in all the world. He gave Megs a hug and said, "We'd better wait around and explain that the Prince is dead. But you're still alive. And that's all I care about at the moment."

Megs gave him a kiss and said, "And you saved my life. You couldn't have done that without the necklace and your own kind heart."

"What's my heart got to do with it?" he whispered in her ear.

"The necklace wouldn't have worked without it," she said. "Look what it did to the Prince."

## EPILOGUE

E d Smith jumped down from the landrover, flushed with the joy of victory. "It's all over!" he shouted. "We've won, but the Prince has vanished!"

The disappearance of the Prince was hard to explain away. When Josh mentioned the snake, Ed's eyes clouded with doubt. "Of course, I believe you," he said, with an unconvincing show of sincerity, "but how am I going to explain that to the troops? People don't turn into snakes – not in the normal world, they don't."

Fortunately, two pirates emerged from the undergrowth to confirm the miracle. They'd been with the Prince, they admitted, but they'd only been following orders. Ed Smith shook them both by the hand and promised them an unconditional pardon for their crimes, providing they stood in front of the troops and confirmed what they had witnessed. Shortly afterwards, an elderly couple, who had stayed in their top-floor apartment throughout the campaign, repeated the story word for word. Then others who'd been watching from their upstairs windows came forward and confirmed what they had seen. Among them was an intrepid journalist who had captured the Prince's last moments on camera.

Of course, the war didn't end just like that. The tale of the Prince's strange death spread slowly through the Western Isles, filling some of his supporters with doubt and dismay. The diehards dismissed the story as propaganda; "they say he was turned into a snake," they protested, "but they never showed us the snake." For others, the tale had the opposite effect. A lot of pirates blamed themselves for turning their backs on the old religion. Chapels sprang up all over the place and pirate priests reported a sudden increase in the size of their congregations. Josh and Megs were not among them.

Peace didn't happen straightaway. The process began in Elephantia and spread slowly through the Western Isles. Colonists who wore circlets had their circlets removed and were fed and cared for in local families and hotels until they were fully fit and had homes to go to. The ring leaders of the pirate uprising were tried by a panel of pirates and colonists. Those that were considered dangerous were imprisoned. The rest – to the anger of many – were set free to return to their homes. Jack Sands set a long-term 'Unity Plan' in place. "If you want to live in peace," he said, "you need to share the same history book. History is a story of quarrels. We only get to hear our own side. But if we want peace we've got to understand the other side's point of view too." He set up a committee of learned historians – both pirates and colonists - whose sole aim was to write a children's history book, explaining all the rights and wrongs that had occurred in the Western Isles since the arrival of the colonists.

Josh and Megs stayed with Josh's parents in the bungalow in Amaryllis and spent much of the time helping each other with their schoolwork and meeting up with old friends. Sandy came over with his parents and stayed for a week in a bungalow a few yards up the road. Sandy had always been interested in mathematics and he had gained the reputation of being a local genius. When he wasn't solving impossible equations, he still liked to go fishing and he and Josh spent much of the time on his dad's fishing boat.

Lavinia came over with her mum for a short stay. Neither of them had much money to spend after Lavinia's grandfather went bankrupt and was shot by a drone, but their fortunes were restored when Lavinia became a famous actress who could be seen almost nightly on the local telescreen. But when she sat chatting with Josh and Megs in the Flagsmith's sitting-room, she was still the forthright and witty girl who'd once walked into Josh's house at the edge of the world.

Josh still kept his necklace because peace and harmony were still far from being restored in the western world, but he'd set his heart on becoming an explorer like his idol, William Feathers. That meant studying hard in some of the subjects he found most difficult – science, geography and history. Megs helped him with his studies because she wanted to accompany him on his adventures, but her chief interest was in medicine. She wanted to become a doctor, like Josh's mum. The two of them paid a short visit to Neustria, where they stayed in the imperial palace with Prunella and Feathers. Prunella dressed up for meetings and special occasions but still spent most of the time in a pink t-shirt and jeans. Feather said she didn't intervene much in meetings but, when she did, she was usually right. She saw problems arising from their decisions that not even the wizard had foreseen.

Josh and Megs travelled a lot in the year that followed the end of the war. They stayed for a few weeks in Josh's old house in Colony Island which still belonged to the Guardian. They met up with Bertie who'd got married and converted his old house into a pub called 'The Smuggler's Rest.' His young wife did most of the cooking and Bertie fattened on the results, as well as printing the menus and managing the accounts. He took Josh and Megs to see the castle of Rupert the Rebel, which the Prince had restored and was now a museum.

After that, they visited Crown Colony which had once been the financial hub of the Western Isles. The island seemed to be creaking back to life, with D.I.Y stores and garden centres supplying the new demand for house building and organic farming. They met Geoffrey Feathers and his young wife, Carol, who proved pretty and charming. She gave a little shiver of alarm, and looked over her shoulder, when she mentioned her step-sister, the cat lady. She was still in prison, she said, but the police were being very kind to her.

They didn't travel to Humphries Island or Windfree. It was still too dangerous in those parts. In any case, they were always glad to return to Amaryllis where Queen Bellagra exercised her eccentric form of 'demogracy.' After all, Josh and Megs were both pirates at heart and always happiest chatting with their friends or alone in one another's company.

*Donald, his wife Joey, and George, the very demanding collie.*

D onald Frank Brown was born in Inverness, Scotland, in 1943 during the second world war. In his gap year, before studying English at Exeter College, Oxford, he worked in Paris selling the New York Times. After teaching English in Brighton and the United Nations school in New York, he settled in Jersey and founded a language school. He is now happily married with three children, ten grandchildren and one great grandchild.

Printed in Great Britain
by Amazon

72473821R00102